ODDS OF LOVE

ODDS OF LOVE

SCANDAL MEETS LOVE 4

DAWN BROWER

"Love looks not with the eyes,
but with the mind,
And therefore is winged Cupid painted blind."

**— WILLIAM SHAKESPEARE, A
MIDSUMMER NIGHT'S
DREAM**

CONTENTS

PROLOGUE

January 1816

Snow trickled down from the sky and blanketed the ground. Lady Katherine Wilson pulled her cloak tighter around her and did her best to

suppress a shiver. The frigid temperature managed to seep underneath the wool cloak and spread over her. She wanted desperately to reach her destination and escape from the cold. She hated winter. It had never been her favorite time of year, and today was no different. It would be better if she could stay home and sit in front of the fire in the sitting room. Even Fortuna's Parlor would be preferable. To be fair each day since her grandmother passed away had been dismal though. What she didn't want to do was visit with solicitors and discuss her loss in depth. Her grandmother was gone. Hadn't she suffered enough already?

She finally reached the offices of her grandmother's solicitor and stepped up to the doorway, and knocked. Katherine had never been to a solicitor before and had no idea what to do. What exactly was the proper protocol when dealing with a solicitor? The finishing school she'd attended hadn't prepared her for this particular circumstance. She probably could have asked Narissa or even Diana, but she hadn't wanted to burden them with her troubles.

The door opened and an older gentleman filled the entryway. He had dark hair with salt and pepper strands streaked through the sides. His dark waistcoat gave him a somber appearance that reflected in his ice blue eyes. Something about him seemed familiar but Katherine couldn't place him in her memory. "Lady Katherine," he greeted her. "Please come in out of the cold."

Had she met him previously? How had he known her at a glance? She would have to inquire during their meeting. "Mr. Adamson?" Katherine lifted a brow. She wanted to make sure he was the solicitor she had a meeting with.

"Yes," he answered as he gestured her past the doorway and closed it behind her.

Katherine shivered. The cold hadn't quite left her even with the warmth that already enveloped her. Sadly, after the conference she'd have to walk home in the awful weather, again. She really wished a carriage had been available to her, but her mother had used it to pay calls.

"Can I take your cloak?" Mr. Adamson asked.

She wanted to keep it on because she was still a little cold; however, soon it would be too warm and it was better to take it off now. Besides she wasn't sure how long their conversation would take. Katherine shrugged the cloak off and handed it to him. He placed it on a nearby hook and then turned toward her. "Follow me. You'll be more comfortable in the office. There's a fire in the hearth and its much warmer."

Mr. Adamson led her to the office and gestured toward a chair. He sat behind a desk and shuffled some papers before glancing back at her. "You're probably wondering why I asked you to meet me here. Normally I'd conduct a visit such as this one in the comfort of the client's home. But because of the nature of your grandmother's last wishes I'm required to do it here. She was afraid that if we met at your father's home he'd try to take control of the assets she left to you. Not that he could have..." He cleared his throat and then continued, "But this makes things simpler for you. There is no conflict to deal with and once you leave you will have control of your inheritance."

What could her grandmother have left for her? She thought her father had inherited all of her grandmother's possessions. Not that Katherine expected her to have much. Most of the estate had already gone to her father when his father passed. It was part of the entailment. Her grandmother lived in a house in Sussex County, near Heathfield. She had always assumed it was the dower house though... "I am not certain I understand."

He handed her a letter. "It is all explained here. You're a very wealthy young lady."

Katherine took the missive from him and broke the seal. "It's from my grandmother..." She recognized her handwriting immediately. Her heart beat heavily in her chest and she fought the urge to cry. She'd been letting her sadness get the best of her for longer than she would have liked. Katherine missed her grandmother terribly.

"Keep reading," Mr. Adamson encouraged her gesturing toward the letter. "It's important you read it until the end."

Katherine turned her attention back to her grandmother's words. What could she have had to say that she couldn't say before she passed away?

My Dearest Grandchild,

Your heart must be heavy, and I'm sorry for the pain you are now feeling. If I could take all your hurt away I would, but if you're reading this then I must no longer be with you. My death, while painful, gives you freedom in ways you probably never imagined. My son, your father, is a harsh man and has not given you the love you need. He learned his behaviors from his own father. My marriage was an arranged one and my mother made assurances that I'd always be provided for. In England, property is immediately owned by a woman's husband after marriage vows are said. My mother didn't believe a woman should be controlled by a man. Love isn't the main requirement in marriage and often doesn't play a part in the contract settlements. That was the case with my own nuptials. A Dukedom such as Gladstone was forged on the bonds of many unions.

5

John was destitute and agreed to all the contractual stipulations before I married him. It was never my desire to become a duchess, but it made my father practically salivate, but I digress.

The important thing you need to understand is that I was never a pawn, and you don't need to be either. My money was controlled by me, but a generous sum was bestowed upon John after we said our vows. He had his money, and I had mine. I provided him with his heir and after that we lived separate lives. Luckily, John didn't waste his money and rebuilt the Gladstone estates. Charles is more his son than mine. Don't let him control you. Seize control of your life.

There are so many things I want to say to you, but the most important last words I can leave you with is this. Marry for love and nothing more. My estate is yours. Use it wisely, my dear. I trust you will make the right decisions. You have the ability to choose your own path now. Happiness can be yours, and love as well.

All my love,
Grandmother

Katherine wiped a tear from her cheek. Her

father wasn't always hard, but she understood what her grandmother meant. Her father wanted to control everything and everyone around him. He hated to be thwarted.

Katherine glanced at Mr. Adamson and asked, "What exactly did my grandmother leave me?"

"As the letter states—her entire estate," he responded matter-of-factly.

"I understand, but what does her estate entail?" She repressed the urge to roll her eyes. "She says I'm wealthy now. Does she mean I have unlimited funds?"

"You do have a sizeable bank account now. There is approximately ten thousand pounds in her account," he answered. "She also left you a horse farm in Sussex. That was your grandmother's main estate and she had a cottage near Bath that you now own. The farm brings in around five thousand pounds per annum"

Katherine's mouth fell open. That was a lot of money... She could do anything she wanted just as her grandmother said in her letter, but Katherine hadn't fully appreciated her words until she heard what she'd inherited. "And my father can't take it away from me?" It was a concern because her father didn't like anyone having more than he did. She couldn't say the state of the dukedom, but that amount of money would surely rival it. He would want it and control of the farm.

"No," he said. "The contracts were clear. Any money she had could only be given to a direct female relation of hers. The only way your father would have inherited it would have been if there were no females to inherit." He lifted his lips upward. "Even then, the first female born of her direct bloodline would gain control of the assets. A male can only retain guardianship of it until a female is born. It's a matriarchal estate."

There were so many possibilities available to her. She wasn't sure what she should do first. Never in her wildest dreams would she have foreseen this happening. Her grandmother's death was the worst and best thing that had ever happened to her. Why hadn't she told her that she'd inherit so much from her? Did she think it would have made a difference in their relationship? Her grandmother had always meant so much to her.

"Is there anything I need to do?" Katherine's mind was still reeling from the news. "Can I go to the farm?"

Her grandmother had always visited her. She'd never been to her estate in Sussex. Katherine had a sudden desire to be amongst her things and the place she loved. It might help her feel closer to her grandmother again. It might be silly, but she needed it.

"There is nothing required of you. Everything has been put into your name. All you need to do is accept your inheritance. If you require anything please let me know and I'll see to it." He slid a stack of papers toward her. "These are for your records. I keep a copy here if they're ever lost and yes, to answer your question, you may visit the farm. If you so desire, you may relocate to Sussex permanently. There's no reason for you to remain at the ducal estate or under your father's care."

That settled it for her. She would go home and pack, then set off for the farm in Sussex. Traveling in winter wasn't her favorite, but to be away from her father would be a blessing. She didn't tell even her closest friends how horrible he could be. Diana and Narissa had no idea how hard it could be for her to sneak out of the house or even to openly gain permission to attend a function. She didn't live the happy-go-lucky life they believed she did. The main reason she'd been looking for a husband was to escape her father's control. Now she didn't have to marry unless she wanted to. She was free to live her life and not worry about anything ever again.

"Thank you so much." Katherine came to her feet. "How soon can I travel there?"

"I can have a carriage ready to take you at any time. When do you wish to go?" He stood and walked around the desk to her side. "The servants already are aware of your ownership and expect you to visit. They're anxious to meet you. They all loved your grandmother."

"I'd like to go at first light tomorrow." Katherine couldn't wait to meet the servants. If they loved her grandmother as she did they'd have much to discuss. "Is that too soon?"

"Not at all," he reassured her. "I'll have a carriage readied. Do you require a chaperone or are you taking your maid with you."

Betty would love to accompany her. She was the only servant in her father's household solely loyal to Katherine. "My maid will be with me." They exited his office and Mr. Adamson retrieved her cloak, then assisted her with it.

"Very well then." He smiled down at her. Where he'd seemed cold to her before he now seemed— almost fatherly, or at least how she imagined a father should be. "Don't forget to let me know if you require anything of me. Safe travels on your journey. I believe you will be pleasantly surprised by the farm. It's a wonderful place. I've visited there often on business for your grandmother."

She'd already thanked him, but it didn't seem like enough. He'd changed her life in the span of less than an hour. Yes, it really was her grandmother that had made her life more bearable, but Mr. Adamson was bearer of that bright news. "I'm sure I'll be fine; however, if something does arise I'll be sure to inform you. Have a good day." Katherine nodded to him and then exited the solicitor's office. For the first time in weeks she walked home with a smile, and not once, even in thought, did she grumble about the cold.

CHAPTER 1

One month later...

The air had a cool crispness to it, but at least it wasn't biting. Katherine sat in the carriage and studied her surroundings. Tattersall's was buzzing with activity. Several gentlemen were already around the yard to view the horses as they were brought out to run around the perimeter of the courtyard. If she wanted to view the horseflesh herself she would have to exit the carriage and join them.

She nibbled on her bottom lip and then took a deep breath. This was what she wanted. Her grandmother had bequeathed her with a horse farm and Katherine was determined to run it all. She wanted to ensure she could be independent and not a young lady society judged. *Her worth would not be determined by a man or her ties to one.* Katherine was determined to stand on her own. Her grandmother had entrusted her with her horse farm and she would do everything she could to ensure it prospered.

She just had to get out of the carriage and brace herself to endure all of the gentlemen's patronizing attitudes. A woman didn't attend Tattersall's auction for the purpose of purchasing horseflesh. She wasn't certain they would even allow her to purchase a horse or well, anything. There were times that being born female was a real disadvantage. At the moment she couldn't think of a time when it was beneficial to be a woman. Katherine sighed and took a deep breath. She pushed open the carriage door and stepped out.

No one stopped to glance in her direction. She took it as a good sign and kept moving forward until she reached the veranda. Tattersall's held its auction outside in a courtyard enclosed on three sides by a wide veranda supported by pillars. Prospective buyers and onlookers gathered in the yard. After everyone was assembled horses would then be released to run around the perimeter. Once that was completed they would then be offered for sale.

Katherine wiped her hands over her light blue wool gown smoothing the fabric, then pulled her cloak tighter around herself to keep out the cold. Then she made sure that the ribbons on her wide bonnet were secured. It would be better for her if she didn't catch anyone's attention. She could make her selections and leave a bank note for payment, then be on her way. The horses she purchases could be delivered to her farm. It all sounded good in theory. The nervous flutter in her stomach suggested that something would go wrong.

She reached the fencing along the perimeter and waited for the horses to be let loose. Wind blew over her face freezing her cheeks. Katherine glanced toward the paddock anxiously. She should have brought her head groom with her. It would still be her decision what horses to buy but having him there would have given her some credibility. Why hadn't she considered that before venturing into Tattersall's?

"Umph." Her breath was knocked out of her as a nearby gentleman knocked her to the side. "Please sir," she said. Katherine couldn't keep the irritation out of her voice. "Pay attention to where you're swinging your arms. You nearly pushed me to the ground." Her side ached where he'd hit her.

"My apologies," the gentleman said. "It wasn't my intention..."

"Of course it wasn't," she chastised him. "Do you always behave so rudely when out in society?"

He lifted a brow. "This isn't exactly society..."

Of course he was right. This was no soiree or ball, but it was still a gathering of high society. Not everyone could afford to buy a horse. She was willing to bet there were more lords at Tattersall's than anyone from the working class. Katherine met the gentleman's gaze and her words froze in her throat. She knew this particular man. It was the Marquess of Holton and she'd been introduced to him while her friend, Diana, now the Countess of Northesk, had been courted by her husband. Katherine had been attracted to the marquess but he'd been rather rude to her during the theater performance they'd been attending at the time. "Lord Holton," she finally managed to force the words out.

He jerked back surprised to hear his name from her. Lord Holton narrowed his gaze and studied her. Her bonnet covered a good deal of her face than she'd intended when she'd donned it earlier this morning. "Lady Katherine?"

She nodded. For a moment there she'd thought he might not remember her. It had to be her bonnet preventing him from fully seeing her face. At least she hoped so. "Yes, my lord."

"What the blazes are you doing at Tattersall's?"

"Well," she began. "Isn't it obvious?" She gestured toward the paddocks. "What does one usually do at a horse auction?"

He frowned. "A lady does not come here to purchase a horse." Lord Holton crossed his arms over his chest. "She sends someone acting on her behalf. What were you thinking coming here? Please tell me you're not alone."

She nibbled on her bottom lip. She couldn't do any such thing. Katherine had come alone and she would not apologize for seizing control of her life. "What if I am?"

He shook his head and his lips formed a fine white line "Does your father know that you are here?"

Her father, the Duke of Gladstone never paid her any attention, at least not any of the good kind. He was controlling but never mean. He doted on his heir, her brother Kendrick and ignored her. When she announced she'd be moving to the horse farm her grandmother had bequeathed her he hadn't cared. At least not once he realized he couldn't seize control of it from her. "My father has more important matters to concern himself than my whereabouts."

Lord Holton scowled. "You need a keeper."

She met his gaze and did not waver once. Allowing this man to browbeat her would only give him the upper hand. Katherine refused to allow him any control over her, no matter how small. "That is a matter of opinion."

The first horse was let out of the paddock to run around the perimeter. Katherine turned away from him and put a little distance between them, but she didn't miss what he'd said under his breath.

"God save him from hellions..."

Well, he need not concern himself with her. She didn't need him to assist her. Katherine was capable of taking care of herself...

BENNETT COULDN'T BELIEVE LADY KATHERINE Wilson was at Tattersall's. The horse auction was not the place for a woman of gentle breeding. Her father should have more care with her reputation and so should she. Lady Katherine might believe it an innocent endeavor but there were far more gentlemen in attendance than ladies and she'd come alone. Her lack of chaperone left her open to scandal and to rogues with lascivious intentions.

He kept her in his sights irritated at the divided intention. Bennett wanted to ignore her, but he couldn't. It wasn't in him to leave a lady in need and whether she realized it or not she did need him. A lady just wasn't safe on her own and somehow he had to ensure she realized that fact. Sir Goliath, the stallion he'd come to view was let out of the paddock to run around the perimeter. He had a fine chestnut coat and a dark black mane. His tail was the same midnight shade as his mane. His muscles rippled as he did a lap around the fenced in area. The horse was beautiful and exactly what he'd been hoping for. He'd bid on him when the auction began.

Lady Katherine had moved a little farther away from him, but that was fine. She was still in his line of sight and close enough he could come to her aid if need be. They let the rest of the horses out of the paddock to run the perimeter but he didn't care. He'd already seen the horse he'd come to view.

After all the horses were finished with their run and everyone had been able to view them they started the auction. Several horses were auctioned off before the stallion came up on the block. Lady Katherine had watched but hadn't bid on anything. Good. She needed to stay out of affairs she didn't belong in.

The bidding started on Sir Goliath. Lady Katherine shouted out her bid surprising Bennett. What the hell... He moved over to her then leaned down and whispered in a harsh tone. "What are you doing?"

"Bidding on the stallion," she said. "I would think that is clear from my shout."

He glared down at her. Her bidding had distracted him from his own intention to obtain the horse. He yelled out a much larger number than the last bidder. Katherine returned his glare and yelled out another bid. "You will not win the horse," he told her. "I will have Sir Goliath."

"I need that horse," she said and pleaded with her eyes. "Don't take him away from me."

He ignored her heartfelt plea. Bennett had wanted that horse before she had even started bidding on Sir Goliath. He wasn't going to outbid her to prevent her from making a mistake, but because it was his intention to win the horse for himself as he'd always intended. After he won the horse he would explain all of that to her. He coveted the horse ever since he had heard about Sir Goliath's line. Bennett intended to race the stallion in the upcoming spring stakes race.

Katherine shouted again hoping to win the horse. He outbid her at every turn. He had the funds to go as high as he wanted. Even though she was the daughter of a duke he doubted she had enough pin money to beat him. He took pleasure in winning. When the auction was over he turned to her with a self-satisfied smile. "You shouldn't have bothered."

She stomped her foot in anger. "You're unscrupulous."

"Darling," he said in a condescending tone. "I saved you from yourself."

"Ohh..." She stomped her foot again. "I hate you. You don't know what you've done, but I can promise you that you did not save me from anything today. You destroyed plans I've been carefully laying down for months now."

"There's no need to make such a fuss. It's one horse. How could me obtaining it instead of you destroy anything?" He lifted a mocking brow. "There are other horses." He gestured to another stallion that was being auctioned as they argued. "That should do for anything you might need."

She lifted her chin defiantly. "No he won't you bloody oaf." Lady Katherine shook her head and stared at him as if she had swallowed something distasteful. "There is only one horse that would work for what I have planned and you took that away from me. I knew you didn't like me much after that night in the theater but I didn't believe you hated me."

"I do not hate you." That would suggest more feelings or thoughts than he'd given to her. She was a lovely chit with dark hair and striking blue eyes, but he hadn't cared one way or the other about her. "I bought the horse because I wanted it. The desire to own it had nothing to do with you. Sir Goliath is going to be a racer."

"I know that you dolt," she seethed with anger. "He's the reason I came to the auction to begin with." Lady Katherine pursed her lips tightly. "I do not require any explanations from you on what a quality horse Sir Goliath is."

She stormed away from him and did not give him another chance to speak. He couldn't help staring at her as she left him standing alone in the courtyard. He still had to settle the payment of Sir Goliath before he could leave. Bennett reassessed his earlier impression of Lady Katherine. He still believed her to be a hellion, but he found he liked her fire. If given the chance he'd take the time to become more acquainted with her. Perhaps he'd pay a call on her and ascertain her reasons for wanting to acquire Sir Goliath. Maybe he could offer her an olive branch of some sort...

Katherine left Tattersall's and went directly to Fortuna's Parlor. She had to be around individuals that supported her and didn't condescend to know what was better for her. She hadn't openly disliked the Marquess of Holton before the auction. Now though... She nearly growled with anger over his high handedness. The last thing she needed was some arrogant male stepping in and trying to control her. Lord Holton might be one of the handsomest lords in the ton, but she would never forget what he'd done to her. She would never look upon him in the same way again.

At one time she thought perhaps he might be a male worth tying herself too. Had even eagerly attended the theater with her friend Diana so she could meet him. He had been polite, yet distant then. It had almost bordered on rude, but she'd allowed him that stance considering they were not acquainted, and he probably had not wanted to encourage her. Some eligible gentlemen didn't want to give a lady the wrong idea. Lord Holton probably had no desire to marry anytime soon. At some point he would have to, but many gentlemen delayed the inevitable as long as they possibly could.

Madame Debroux's modiste shop was at the front of where Fortuna's Parlor was located, and she didn't want to disturb her or her customers. When she reached the shop, she checked around her before she went to the rear and entered Fortuna's. This time of day there wasn't a lot of activity in the all-women's gaming hell run by Lady Narissa, the Duchess of Blackmore. Lady Lulia, the Duchess of Clare usually could be found in one of the backrooms giving fencing lessons. There was a good chance that Lady Diana, the Countess of Northesk would be there too. They were all dear friends of hers and she desperately needed to be with at least one of them. Even the Duchess of Blackmore would do even though she wasn't quite as close to her as she was the others.

Katherine practically ran up the stairs until she

reached the door that led into the club. She pushed the door open and stepped inside. There were more people there than she had expected. The door to Narissa's office was open. She peeked inside and noticed the duchess busy working at her desk. A ledger of some sort was open, and she stared down at it. Her dark hair was pulled back into an elegant chignon and she nibbled on her bottom lip. A strikingly handsome man stood by her side—the Duke of Blackmore, Narissa's husband had come to the club with her. Not that he didn't ever come to Fortuna's, but it was rare. She must need his advice on something...

She left them to look over the books and headed to the back room. Lulia was indeed in the room, but she wasn't giving lessons to a new student. Diana was fencing with her though she probably shouldn't be. If her husband knew he'd have her hide. Diana was pregnant with their first child. She was easily three months into her pregnancy. Katherine stepped into the room and glared at the two of them, but they both ignored her. They continued to parry back and forth until Diana lunged forward and pushed the blunt end of her foil against Lulia's shoulder. "I win," she declared in a triumphant voice.

"You did," Lulia agreed. Her accent hinted

toward her gypsy roots. "Though I doubt you would have if I did not go easy on you." She chuckled lightly.

They both turned to Katherine and flashed matching happy grins at her. Diana took her fencing equipment off and set them to the side. She walked over to Katherine and embraced her in a welcoming hug. "What do we owe the honor of your presence. I thought you were at your new horse farm."

Katherine sighed. "I came into town to attend the auction at Tattersall's." She frowned at the memory of that awful experience again. "I should not have tried to bid on a horse myself."

"Oh dear," Diana said sympathetically. "What happened."

Lulia, who had also taken off her equipment, retrieved Diana's and put them all away in the large cedar chest she used to store them, then came over to join them. Katherine waited until she reached their sides until she spoke again. "Lord Holton is an arrogant prig."

Lulia chuckled. "I've met the man and I couldn't agree more. He stifles poor Lenora. I've tried to befriend her and have even invited her to visit me in Tenby when we are not in town. She's yet to take me up on the offer. Fin and I will be returning to his family home soon." She gestured toward Diana. "It's the only reason I gave in to her need to fence. When I return, she'll be as big as a house and unable to move properly."

Diana glared at her cousin. Lulia's father was Diana's father's brother. They just realized they were related recently but had been friends long before that. "There's no need to be rude."

"I only speak the truth," she said, her accent thick as she spoke the words. "I'm certain you'll have your lovely trim figure back in no time after the babe's birth."

Diana crinkled her nose up in displeasure at Lulia's statement and then rubbed her belly her face brightened into a soft smile. "Either way I have no regrets. I welcome this child and all it will bring me."

Katherine envied her friends. They both had found love and were going to all have a family soon. She'd feel like the odd one out when she was with them, but she'd never wish anything different for them. She turned to Lulia. "Will you be adding to your family now that you've married the duke?"

Horror spread over Lulia's face. "You think I would make a good mother?"

Katherine laughed at Lulia's outrage. "You would. Of all of us you'll be the best mother. You're like that with us. Always guiding us in the direction we should go without us realizing it at the time. You're more nurturing than any woman I'm acquainted with." Lulia had helped guide Diana toward the earl, and she didn't doubt she'd do the same for Katherine if she found the man she was supposed to be with.

"That may be so," Lulia agreed. "But you are all grown up and only take minimal care. A child..." She shuddered. "They would require much more than I believe I am capable of." Lulia let out a breath. "Though, I suppose, at some point I should consider giving Fin an heir. He is a duke after all and his title will have to pass down to someone..."

"There is that," Diana said with a sly smile. "And it would be nice for my little one to have some cousins to grow with."

"Don't give Fin any ideas," Lulia said. "He'll use that against me later." She let out a light laugh. "Though it wouldn't take much for him to convince me. There isn't much I wouldn't do for that man. He hasn't pushed though and I love him all the more for it. If it happens, it happens. I may say I don't want a child, but all children are blessings. It would be a gift to have a babe that was a mix of me and my love."

Katherine's heart hurt listening to them both.

She'd come to Fortuna's to complain about losing out on a horse. Now she was starting to see how trivial her problems were. She wanted much more than that for herself. The horse farm was lovely, but she desired...well, what Diana and Lulia had. "Whatever child either one of you have will be lucky to have you as their mother."

Lulia smiled. "We have lost track of the conversation. What happened at Tattersall's and what did Lord Holton do?"

"I went there to purchase a stallion," Katherine began. "He will be a good racehorse and I had hoped to breed him with a couple of my mares—produce more racehorses..."

"That is a fantastic idea," Diana exclaimed. "Narissa could even ride them for you.

"I had hoped to discuss that with her later," Katherine admitted.

Lulia narrowed her gaze. "Lord Holton outbid you didn't he?" She sighed. "He has more funds than he knows what to do with. Did he actually want the stallion or did he obtain it to spite you?"

Katherine blew out a breath. "He says he wanted the horse for himself, but I have my doubts. He chastised me the entire time for daring to attend the auction to begin with. I needed that horse..."

"I didn't realize Lord Holton was interested in racehorses," Diana said. "Perhaps we can pay a call on Lenora. She might know more."

Katherine didn't care either way. Lord Holton believed that he was saving her from herself. Even if he didn't want the horse for himself he'd never sell it to her now. "I don't know what good that would do. I would hate to cause Lady Lenora any stress..." She barely knew Lord Holton's cousin, Lady Lenora St. Martin. She'd only spoken to her a few times.

"I do not think Lenora has any sway over Lord Holton," Lulia said. "But I think we can, or at least you can, use the visit for other reasons. Don't press Lenora for information, but go at a time Lord Holton is home. You can corner him and make him listen to you."

"I don't understand," Katherine said.

"You want to use the horse as a stud correct?" Lulia asked.

"Yes," Katherine replied.

"Then ask him to loan the horse to you—for a fee of course. You get to breed your horses with it and he can keep his racehorse. That's a win-win for you. You can start building your stock with a stud fee and you don't have the upkeep of the horse."

Katherine hadn't thought about that. Something

told her that it would take a lot to convince Lord Holton of the wisdom of that plan. He didn't seem the type to want to work with a woman who owned a horse farm. She might have to be sneakier than that. Lord Holton might respond better if he dealt with another male. She'd have to discuss it with her stable master when she returned to the farm.

"I know you like the direct approach," she told Lulia. "But Lord Holton doesn't think a woman should do anything outside the norms society sets for them. I might need your help later with a much sneakier plan."

Lord Holton would rue the day he ever decided to get in Katherine's way. She would show him a woman was capable of anything. If possible, she would strive to change his mind and attitude toward women in general. A woman could do anything, or well just about anything, if she chose to.

"I'll do what I can." Lulia's lips curled into a devious smile. "It will be fun to ruffle that man's feathers a bit. I'll do my part to achieve that goal.

"Good," Katherine said. The plan was already starting to take shape in her mind.

"I'll help if I can too," Diana said. "I'm sorry he's made building on your stable more difficult."

"I'm glad I decided to visit Fortuna's before I

with a glass of brandy in his hand. Northesk sat to his right with a stack of cards in his hand. Bennett strolled over and took the seat to Ashley's left. "Are you preparing for a game?" He gestured toward the cards in Northesk's hand.

Northesk shuffled the cards with expert precision. "We considered it but it's no fun with two people. Even with you here we're missing a fourth."

"We can try..." Bennett started to suggest playing a different game, but he wasn't sure what would work.

"No," Ashley interrupted him.

Bennett closed his mouth and shook his head. It was a halfhearted effort either way. He wasn't sure he wanted to play a game of any sort. He was still rather irritated from the auction at Tattersall's. "I suppose you'd prefer getting foxed instead." He lifted a brow.

"I'd prefer not to start something guaranteed to induce uncontrollable ennui." The duke's languor tone hinted he'd already drifted toward boredom. "I suppose imbibing too much brandy might help us forget for a while."

"Forget what?" Northesk asked.

"That we live such tedious lives, of course." Ashley drained the glass in one gulp and then waved to a nearby servant. "Bring a couple bottles of brandy, then leave us alone."

"Right away, Your Grace," the servant said and then bowed before he left to do Ashley's bidding.

"You really do plan on getting snockered, don't you?" Bennett said as he raised a brow. Bennett never overindulged. He hadn't been gifted that luxury. From and early age he'd had to assume control of the family estate. There were a lot of hard lessons learned as he stumbled through everything. He had been a mere eight and ten years when his father had passed. Not enough time to acclimate himself to the responsibilities of life. Though to be fair he never would have been prepared for the loss of his father. Even with that loss he'd never turned to liquor of any sort. He didn't understand how some individuals could lose themselves in a bottle. Bennett liked Brandy, but in moderation.

"Do you have a better suggestion?" Ashley asked.

Bennett opened his mouth to explain exactly what they could do but promptly closed it. What would he gain from listing possible entertainments? Ashley always did as he pleased anyway.

"Don't encourage him," Northesk said. "He's been in a foul mood since we arrived."

He glanced at the earl and told him, "I'd already decided against it.

The waiter brought the bottles of brandy that Ashley had requested and set them on the table. "Will you require anything else?" he asked.

Ashley waved his fingers in a dismissive manner. "No. Leave us."

The Duke of Clare strolled into the room and sat in the empty chair. He glanced between them and said, "Am I interrupting?"

Northesk shuffled the cards again. "Not at all." He gestured toward Bennett and Ashley. "We were considering a game of whist. Are you interested?"

"Speak for yourself," Ashley said. "I plan on drinking lots and lots of brandy." He tilted his head to the side. "I suppose I can suffer through a game or two though if Clare is willing."

"I..." Clare stumbled over his words. "Suppose..."

Bennett sighed. He wasn't at all certain what he'd hoped to accomplish when he came to the club. Ashley and Northesk were his closest mates. Clare was a decent sort, but he didn't know him well. He studied Clare and then glanced at Northesk. They were married to females acquainted with Lady Katherine. Perhaps they might give him a little insight on the lady's motivations. He first turned toward the earl and asked, "How familiar are you with Lady Katherine Wilson?"

"She visits with Diana often," he answered. "Seems like a pleasant sort. She attended the theater with us in your box that one time."

Ah yes... He did recall that. They hadn't gotten on well that night. Lady Katherine had tried to make small talk with him as was polite, but Bennett had wanted to pay attention to the play. "What is her family situation?" Perhaps he should apprise her father of her activities. Though something told him that it wouldn't do any good. Her father must not have much control over her for her to believe it was all right to attend the auction at Tattersall's on her own.

"Why do you ask?" Northesk inquired and started to deal the cards. It appeared as if they didn't have much choice. They were about to embark in a game of whist.

Bennett sighed. He should have known it wouldn't be a simple endeavor. Instead of telling him what was bothering him he said, "I was able to purchase the stallion at Tattersall's this afternoon."

"Sir Goliath?" Ashley sat forward. "The one you hope to race?"

"The very one?"

"What does the stallion have to do with Lady Katherine?" the Duke of Clare asked in an innocuous tone.

He had hoped to change their topic of conversation. Trust the Duke of Clare to stumble on the one subject he hadn't wanted to discuss. There was no helping it now. Ashley would pick up on it and not let it go for anything—he'd be even worse the more inebriated he became. Northesk would be more subtle about it, but even he would ask questions.

"Apparently she hoped to attain the stallion for herself," he finally answered. "Though I can't fathom why a lady of her stature would require a stallion like Sir Goliath."

"She was at the auction?" Northesk asked.

"Yes."

"By herself?" The earl shook his head bewilderment filling his eyes. "Somehow that doesn't surprise me. None of the ladies of my wife's acquaintance are...normal."

"I should probably take offense to that," the Duke of Clare stated blandly. "Considering my wife is one of her intimates, but you're not far off. What makes Lulia different is what made me fall in love with her to begin with."

None of that was assisting him in discovering

what Lady Katherine's motivations were. "So neither one of you is aware of why she might want Sir Goliath?" It bothered him far more that it should. She had acted as if he had wronged her gravely.

The Duke of Clare shrugged. "Lulia might know. Lady Katherine has been visiting her often. Then there is that club..."

"What club?" Bennett asked. "Is there a place the women go to gather and complain about those that do them wrong? Or is it more like a quartet where they practice music?"

"Like a sewing circle?" the Duke of Ashley supplied and laughed. "Have you met those ladies? None of them would do anything so sedate."

Northesk burst into laughter and then picked up his cards. "He is right. Diana has a lot invested in that club and as far as I can tell they all do. Lulia and Diana also fence almost daily. She thinks I don't know that and I let her believe I'm oblivious."

"Why would you do that?" Bennett asked disconcerted. "She's putting herself and the child she's carrying in danger." He'd never allow his wife to do anything of the sort.

"Because I trust her to do what's best for herself and our child. If I demanded she stopped she'd be reckless. This keeps the peace and allows her a sense of freedom." He smiled. "That and Lulia is more overprotective of her than I ever could be. She'll make sure Diana doesn't do anything foolish."

The Duke of Clare picked up his cards and stared at them. "My wife has been keeping you informed of her activities hasn't she?"

"Not exactly," Northesk replied. "She only said she'd make sure I was aware of anything that might prove too dangerous for her. We have an understanding."

All of this had Bennett's head swimming. He picked up his cards and stared at them—not really seeing them. Ashley picked up his cards after he took another swig of brandy. "Are we playing or gossiping like old biddies."

They started the game but Bennett barely paid attention. Somehow he didn't manage to blunder. His thoughts kept straying to Lady Katherine. He didn't know what to do about her. He felt as if he owed her something. Bennett may not have liked her attending the auction, but he'd never wanted to harm her in any fashion. Why would she need that stallion? What did she hope to gain by owning the horse? He would have to call on her and ask a few probing questions. Only then he could ascertain a way to make reparations.

He turned toward Clare and asked, "When do you return to your estate?" The Duke of Clare didn't like being in London longer than he had to be, but Lulia didn't like being far away from Diana.

"When Northesk here retires to his estate Lulia and I will return to Tenby," he answered. "Probably a little sooner. I have to meet with my estate manager and some of the tenants."

He nodded his head absentmindedly. Did Lady Katherine return to her father's estate or did she remain in London. What did she do when the duchess and the countess were not in town? Did she have any other acquaintances she spent time with? There was so much he didn't know about her. "I'm going to have to do the same soon." He threw a card on the table and the other gentleman did as well.

"I'm not," Ashley said. "I leave that to the people I hired to oversee it all. Too much stress running everything."

"One day you will have to take the mantle," Northesk said. "We all do." Not that long ago Northesk buried himself in a bottle quite regularly. Falling in love with Diana helped put him on a better path.

"But not today," Ashley said and placed his last

card on the table. "I believe that I come out ahead. What do I win?"

"Another bottle of brandy?" Bennett offered. Ashley didn't need money.

"Send it to my townhouse," Ashley announced. "I'm going to visit my mistress." He stood up and left the three of them alone in the room.

"I'm worried about him," Northesk said quietly.

"I am as well," Bennett admitted. "But what are we to do? He's got to find a way out of this mood of his on his own. Probably won't snap out of it until he's ready to settle down with a wife."

Northesk sighed. "You're right. You usually are." He was quiet a moment. "Don't think I didn't notice you're preoccupied. I'm not certain what happened between you and Lady Katherine, but go easy on her. She's in mourning. Her grandmother passed on a few months ago and she took it hard."

That was more information than he'd had previously. "I'll take that under advisement."

The Duke of Clare stood. "If you'll excuse me I'm going to go home to my wife." He bowed and left Bennett and Northesk alone.

"It's time I went as well. Diana is expecting me."

Bennett nodded. "Go. When you have a moment

come take a look at Sir Goliath. He's as gorgeous as stated."

"Will do," Northesk said as he stood. "I'll send word around when I have time to visit your stables. Good day." He nodded and left Bennett alone.

Bennett sighed and stared across the table. Both bottles of brandy were empty. He hadn't realized how steadily Ashley had been drinking. Maybe it was time for them to step in and help him take a different path. The question was: would he allow it? He would ponder the situation later. First he would uncover Lady Katherine's secrets and ascertain what he could do to assist her. There had to be a way to soothe her ruffled feathers...

CHAPTER 4

*H*yde Park was brimming with activity for a winter day. A slightly chilly breeze blew over them as they strolled along the walking path of the park. Katherine was on Diana's left and Lulia on her right as they moved through the path. Katherine didn't feel very social. She hadn't found the opportunity to visit Lenora and therefore she hadn't been able to approach Lord Holton about using his horse as a stud. It was a delicate subject and she didn't believe he would be open to the possibility. At least not with her... If she'd been born male he'd have taken her far more seriously. As it was he didn't think her capable of doing simple tasks let alone run a horse farm. Not that he was aware of her venture or her inheritance. In her mind that wasn't any of his concern. Now though, she had to broach the topic with him if she had any hopes of continuing forward.

"You're awfully quiet today," Diana said to Katherine.

She nibbled on her lip pensively. "Am I?"

"You know you are," Lulia said. Her gypsy accent thick as she spoke the words. "Are you still bothered by Lord Holton purchasing Sir Goliath? Have you seen him since?"

What Lulia wanted to know was had Katherine acted upon the duchesses' idea of asking Lord Holton to breed Sir Goliath with a couple of Katherine's mares.

"I haven't had the opportunity," she admitted aloud. "I'm not certain I will either. I return to the farm tomorrow. I've already stayed in London longer than I planned."

"Have you spoken to Narissa?" Diana asked.

That was one of the things she still had to do before she left London. The Duchess of Blackmore was an expert in racehorses and had ridden several herself. She could help her train the horses and if not ride them herself, recommend someone to her. "I am going to visit Fortuna's later today."

"Don't wait too long to approach Lord Holton,"

Lulia said. "You must not allow him to prevent you from achieving your goals."

Katherine would not roll her eyes. Not because it was unlady like, but because she did respect Lulia. The duchess was hardly ever wrong. Katherine just didn't want to discuss anything of import with the marquess. Lord Holton had been so derisive with her. She didn't relish the idea of being treated as inferior because of her gender. "I promise I will not give him the opportunity to prevent me from doing what I wish." Not that he had control over her actions to begin with. He wasn't anything to her. Even if he denied her the use of his horse as a stud she could always find another way to move forward. "I could always find another horse to breed my mares with." They just wouldn't be as good as Sir Goliath...

"You could," Lulia agreed. "But why when you can have the one you wanted to begin with." She nodded to her left. "And here is the perfect occasion to test the waters."

Katherine glanced in the direction that Lulia had gestured. Lord Holton rode in a phaeton with his cousin Lady Lenora St. Martin. They had stopped to talk with another carriage. Katherine narrowed her gaze to see who was in the other carriage and sighed. It was the Duke and Duchess of Blackmore. Well...

She could complete two tasks at once. It would save her a trip to Fortuna's later.

Lulia didn't give her the chance to change her mind. She looped her arm through Diana's and Katherine's and led them over to the two carriages. When they reached the carriages Narissa noticed them first. "Lady Northesk, Lady Katherine, Your Grace," she greeted them all.

"Your Grace," the three of them said in unison. They were outside of Fortuna's and kept up appearances. If they were at their gaming hell they'd have dropped all formalities.

Lord Holton's mouth formed a firm white line. He had pinned his gaze upon Katherine and it had not unwavered since they approached. Apparently he still held a grudge. Katherine braced herself for some sort of upbraiding from the marquess. If he were going to be difficult she'd at least give him further reason to do so. She pasted a smile on her face and boldly met his gaze. "Lord Holton how good to see you again."

He pulled his eyebrows together questioningly. "It is?"

"Indeed," she said. "It's quite fortuitous. I had hoped to speak with Lady Blackmore later this afternoon, but since you're both here…"

Narissa's smile widened almost as if she knew exactly what Katherine wished to discuss with her. "You must join us in the carriage." She motioned for the three of them to sit across from her and her husband. The duke stepped out of the carriage to assist them into the carriage. Once they were all seated again Narissa turned to Katherine. "What did you wish to discuss?"

"It's about a horse." Katherine's lips twitched a little as Lord Holton's gaze hardened.

"A particular horse?" Narissa asked.

"Partially," Katherine answered. "I had plans to expand on the breeding stock at the farm."

"I take it by the past tense term that you no longer do?" Narissa raised a brow. "Did something happen to alter your course?"

"Indeed," Katherine replied. "But I had hoped to still go forward with the help of Lord Holton." She turned toward the marquess. Surprise etched across his face.

"I'm afraid I do not understand what it is you wish from me," he said slowly.

Lord Blackmore chuckled softly and his wife pressed her elbow into his side. "What?" he asked.

"Keep your thoughts to yourself," she chastised him.

"I didn't say..."

"You were thinking it loudly," Narissa said.

The duke shook his head but kept his lips sealed. Katherine held back a grin. She suspected the duke had heard about the incident at Tattersall's but she couldn't be certain. It was the only reason she could think that he'd have openly chuckled as he had. Instead of pressing that issue she returned her attention to Lord Holton. "Would you consider allowing me to use Sir Goliath as a stud?"

"Pardon me?" he asked taken aback. "You want..." He nearly choked on the words. "To give you my horse to breed with what? Your pony?"

Katherine rolled her eyes. She couldn't stop herself even if she wanted to. "For a fee of course." She took a deep breath. "And no, my lord, I wouldn't breed a stallion with a pony. I have some retired racing stock. Two gorgeous mares that if bred properly could produce some more racehorses."

"You..." He paused and then continued as if aghast at the very thought of it. "Breed horses?"

He shook his head several times. He really was having difficulty stomaching the idea that Katherine dared to do something so masculine. "Indeed," she answered. "I inherited a horse farm from my grandmother and I've been building on the stock and making minor repairs and expansions to the farm where needed. Breeding the racehorses is a new venture that I believe will be quite profitable." She turned to Narissa. This was where the duchess came in. "You're more experienced than I am with racing. I had hoped you would come to the farm and inspect the mares and help me with raising the new horses when they're born. Maybe even ride them..." It would be some time before the foals would be able to be ridden, but she believed the duchess would have an interest in them.

"Oh..." She put her hand up to her chest. "That's...oh, yes, I certainly would. Can I have first pick? I've been hoping to get a new horse to race and it would be wonderful if I had a hand in raising it."

"Absolutely," Katherine agreed. "Though it does depend a little on Lord Holton. He purchased Sir Goliath and I had hoped to use the stallion to breed the mares with."

Narissa turned her attention to the marquess. "Surely you don't have issue with Sir Goliath begetting a couple foals?" She lifted her brow high. "You can still race him and allow him to be used as a stud."

Lulia patted Katherine's knee. Her and Diana had remained quiet through the entire exchange allowing her to dive in and corner Lord Holton. Lady Lenora's shyness kept her buried against the carriage next to her cousin. She was famously timid and it was a shame. Lord Holton's eyes thundered with rage, but he kept it leashed tightly. Katherine was amazed he remained cool-headed considering. He probably hated being put upon as she'd done. He took a deep breath and said. "We can discuss the fee for using Sir Goliath as a stud later." He'd probably try to find a way not to hold to his end of the deal.

"Wonderful," Katherine said. "I'm returning to the farm in the morning. I'll send direction before I depart and you can write when you wish to discuss terms."

She had him and she wouldn't let him slither away. Katherine so needed a win, when she'd been feeling a little down lately. She turned toward Narissa. "I'll send you a missive once I'm certain that the breeding took. When the foals are born you may wish to come inspect them." She wasn't sure how amiable Lord Holton would be about allowing her to use Sir Goliath as a stud more than this one time. She'd have to take full advantage of it while she could.

"That's perfect." Narissa's grin widened. She nodded at Lord Holton. "It was generous of you to agree. It's a wonderful thing you're doing helping out Lady Katherine carve out her independence."

He was taken aback at her words. "I didn't realize Lady Katherine sought independence of any sort. I'm glad I was able to do my part and assist her on that endeavor."

"It's a kind gesture, my lord," Lady Katherine said politely. She didn't believe for one second that he would have aided her in any other circumstance. He didn't think a lady should do anything outside of what the standards society had set for her.

"Do you wish to continue to ride with us?" the duke asked. "Or would you rather finish your stroll."

"A carriage ride sounds lovely," Diana answered for them both. "I suddenly find myself fatigued."

Diana placed her hand over her stomach area. The baby growing inside of her drained the momentum out of the countess more often than not. She wasn't far along in her pregnancy either. It would probably worsen as she got farther along. Then she'd be tired dealing with an infant daily. Lulia smiled softly at Diana and said, "Then it's agreed. We will ride more with the duke and duchess." She turned toward them. "Do you mind dropping us off at the Northesk townhouse? Diana's probably going to want to rest later."

"Of course," the duke answered readily. He nodded at Lord Holton. "I'll see you later at the club." Then he flicked the reins and set the horsed in motion. They remained quiet for the rest of the journey. When they reached the townhouse the duke stepped out to assist the ladies out of the carriage.

Diana yawned almost immediately after her feet hit the ground. "I don't know why I'm so tired..."

"Don't think too hard on it. You'll hurt your head," Lulia told her. She faced the duke and said, "Thank you for bringing us here."

"It was my pleasure," he replied and then bowed to them. "Ladies have a pleasant afternoon." He then turned on his heels and joined his wife in the carriage, and then they were off. Probably returning to their own home.

"I'll leave the two of you as well," Katherine told Lulia and Diana. "There are a few things I wish to do before I depart tomorrow." At least one of them was no longer talking with Narissa about her racehorse ideas. "I'll write when I have the opportunity."

"Please do," Lulia said. "I do wish to discover how well your venture does." She had one of her knowing smiles on her face. Katherine didn't like it.

Lulia tended to perceive more than the average person.

Katherine didn't bother to respond to her though. She just nodded and then headed away from her two friends. Only time would tell how her venture actually did. She hoped that Lord Holton didn't find a way to back out of allowing her to use Sir Goliath to breed with her mares.

CHAPTER 5

A fortnight later...

Katherine pulled out a chair in her chambers and sat down. She had to go out to inspect the horses and see that everything was going well in the stables. She'd never have believed living on a horse farm would help her find a sense of belonging. The inheritance her grandmother had left her opened up a world of possibilities. She had something that was solely hers and she could do whatever she chose to. That sense of freedom had been missing from her life and Katherine found she'd do almost anything to hold on to it.

So far everything she'd sought out to do had gone well. The one failure still sparked a sense of rage inside of her. Lord Holton hadn't responded to the missive she'd sent him outlining the plans she had for using Sir Goliath as a stud. Katherine had hoped he would follow through and allow her to use the horse. So far though he had done everything but and she didn't think he would ever deign to let her near Sir Goliath. It was too bad really. She'd have to find a different horse to start her racehorse-breeding program. There were other horses that would work. She had just hoped to use Sir Goliath above all else.

She pulled on her boots and secured them in place, then stood. She smoothed down her skirts and went to pull on her riding jacket. After she was done inspecting the horses she planned on riding the farm's perimeter. There were more than stables and horses to keep the farm running smoothly. She had an overseer that went around the farm regularly, but Katherine liked to have a pulse on the property herself. She was still learning but she wasn't going to get proficient if she didn't make an effort.

Katherine stepped out of her chambers and descended the stairs. She was pulling her gloves on as she walked out the door and nearly ran right into a hard male chest. She stopped short as she pulled the rest of her glove on. Lord Holton was on her front step. What was he doing there? Had he come to discuss Sir Goliath in person? A letter would have worked just as well...

"Lady Katherine," he greeted and bowed. "I hope I haven't caught you at an inopportune time."

"Not at all, my lord," she answered. "If you don't mind walking with me I'm about to go to the stable." It was a good time for her as long as he didn't make anything more difficult than it needed to be. She could show off her farm to him and maybe, just maybe, entice him to join her venture a little.

He fell into step beside her as they walked briskly toward the stable. "Your farm is quite...large," he said.

"That surprises you?" What was he trying to say with that pronouncement? Katherine didn't understand the marquess at all.

"No..." He cleared his throat. "I didn't know what to expect when I decided to visit."

"Why did you?"

"Did I what?" He tilted his head to the side and stared at her.

Katherine stopped and faced him. He nearly stumbled as he halted with her. "Come here of course?" She sighed. "Surely you understand it wasn't necessary for you to visit the farm. Any business we partake in could have been handled via missive."

"I don't like to become embroiled in any venture without fully inspecting all aspects and studying every part of it in detail. I do not know if this is a good risk or not without at the very least visiting the farm."

She lifted a brow. "Are you mad?"

"Of course not," he said a little affronted. "What makes you believe something so preposterous?"

"Because what you just described doesn't remotely apply to our situation. The only business we will embark upon is your horse impregnating my mares. That is the long and short of it. I'll pay you for the use of your horse and that precludes the arrangement. You don't need to study my farms to determine if it is a good venture."

"Of course I do," he said. "How else am I to determine if my horse will be safe while it is in your care?"

She would not roll her eyes. She wouldn't. God she wanted to. "What do you expect I'll do with Sir Goliath while he is here? I'm certainly not the one hoping to breed with him."

He opened his mouth and closes it several times like a fish out of water. Lord Holton pursed his lips tightly together as he struggled to control his outrage. After several heartbeats he started to speak. "A lady doesn't discuss crude topics such as breeding."

"Then how every am I supposed to find a stud for my mares?" She shook her head exasperated. "I believe it is safe to assume that you and I are not going to agree on anything, my lord. What do I need to do to gain your agreement? I really would like to breed my mares with Sir Goliath."

"The Duke of Blackmore visited me a few days ago. He came to inquire as to the progress of the possible breeding." He drew his eyebrows together. "Did you ask about it in the duchess's presence for the sake of forcing my hand?"

She hadn't sought to do that to begin with, but she did take advantage of a fortuitous situation. "That was just a happy accident."

"Happy for you anyway..."

"I don't deny that." She smiled. "Is the duchess pushing through her husband to get what she desires?"

"The duke strongly suggested I visit the farm and decide afterward. So I'm here. Show me your farm and convince me of the wisdom of breeding your mares with my stallion."

It was an audition of sorts. She wasn't an actress

hoping to play the lead role on stage, but it was a role of sorts. She had to paly a part that would entice Lord Holton. Well then so be it. She'd find some balance between the lady he believed she should be and the independent woman she hoped to achieve.

BENNETT KEPT BLUNDERING NO MATTER WHAT he said. Lady Katherine seemed determined to disagree with him on every matter. He'd never met a lady like her and he wasn't certain how to handle her. She was smart, determined, and stubborn as hell. Why had he let the Duke of Blackmore convince him that visiting the farm was a good idea? The horse farm was two day's ride outside of London. He'd have to find an inn to stay at in the evening. Riding back at night wasn't a good idea. Not with highwaymen scattered along the roads ready to pounce at the first opportunity.

Lady Katherine stared at him as if he wasn't worth her time. She had her mouth in a firm line and her cheeks were reddened. He wasn't sure if it was from the brisk wind or anger heating her cheeks. He suspected it might be a combination of both. She sighed and then nodded at him. "Very well, my lord.

I'll give you a tour of my estate. We will start in the stables and then if you wish you can accompany me as I ride the perimeter and make sure the fences are all intact."

"Don't you have an estate manager that handles that?" He lifted a brow. "That's not..."

"Please don't finish that sentence, my lord. This is my estate, not yours. If you wish to allow someone other than yourself to ensure the running of your estate is done correctly, that is your decision. I prefer to view my lands whenever possible so I can make sound choices that will help my property prosper."

"I didn't say that..." He made another mistake. Nothing he did with her was right. "I do inspect my property."

"Then you agree it isn't a task that should be associated with a gender?" She tilted her head. "It is my property and therefore my responsibility."

He sighed. "You're correct. If you don't have a male you can trust then yes, you should inspect it."

"What if I did have a male I could trust?" She glared at him. "Then I shouldn't bother? What if I want to? Doesn't my wishes make any difference with you?"

She was determined to fight with him. He should just keep his mouth closed and not bother to find some kind of commonality for them to discuss. She wouldn't allow any peace to be brokered between them. He'd left her with a horrible impression and she didn't seem inclined to alter it for any reason. "My lady," he began. "Do you wish to have Sir Goliath used as a stud here? If you have changed your mind please tell me now and I will leave immediately. I do not wish to take you away from your responsibilities and misuse the time I've allowed for this visit if it isn't your desire."

She blew out a breath and then clenched her teeth together. He'd struck her wrong with those words. Lady Katherine did indeed want to breed her mares with Sir Goliath. If she wanted to do so she'd have to find a way to rein in her temper. "Very well," she said. "I'll quit being so combative. My apologies, my lord. Please follow me into the stable."

They started walking again and went into the stable. The stables were in pristine condition. There were hay bales stacked on one side of the stable. The opposite had several straw bales. Bags of oats leaned against the hay. For a stable, it was relatively clean. The horses had plenty of water and food for them. "Where do they get their exercise?"

"We have several fenced in pastures for them," she answered. "They are on a rotation and the stable master takes them out to pastures to run. Some of them are ridden by stable hands for more extensive and practiced exercise."

"I see," he said quietly. "This seems really well organized."

"You sound surprised again, my lord."

He was. Bennett didn't think he would ever be able to organize something this well. He was rather meticulous with all his business ventures and he wouldn't have been this good with a horse farm. At least he didn't believe he would be, but running a horse farm hadn't ever been something he had hoped to do. "Pleasantly so," he agreed. "I think Sir Goliath would do well in this stable. Probably better than my stables."

"I do like to give the horses the best life they can have, outside of being free that is. There is only so much I can do to give them the illusion of being free to do as they please. I must keep them if I'm to make a profit. And well, I doubt they'd do well on their own."

"Not after being in captivity," he agreed.

"So you'll allow me the use of Sir Goliath?"

"We can iron out the terms of his use. Then I'll have the contracts drawn to be signed. After that... Yes, I think that I can allow him to be used as a stud."

She smiled at him. "Thank you, my lord. Do you care to join me as I inspect the property?"

"Yes," he said. "As we ride we can discuss the terms if that is all right with you."

"It is," she agreed.

They walked over to one of the stable hands and Lady Katherine directed him to have two horses saddled. He watched her as she gave orders. He found her more intriguing than he wanted to admit. She had a lovely heart shaped face, soft pink lips, and high cheekbones. Her midnight tresses were bound high up on her head, but tiny tendrils escapes to curl around her face and down her neck. He wanted to yank her hair free to see if it was as silky soft and he thought it to be. Bennett shook that thought away. This was not the time or the place for such musings. Lady Katherine wasn't for him. But he certainly did want her....

CHAPTER 6

A sennight later...

Katherine stood in the fenced in pasture next to one of her chestnut mares. She held a brush in her left hand and ran in along the horse's mane and then moved over to the mare's back. For her it was a peaceful task and it allowed her to ponder over some of the farm's issues as she stroked the horse with a brush. Sammy was a good girl and had a pleasant disposition. She wasn't one of the mares she wanted to breed for racing, but she would probably still breed her for a different sort of horse. Carriage and riding horses were always in need and they kept the farm flush with working capital.

Lord Holton had left to ponder over her proposal. She still wasn't certain he would agree to it, but she had hope. More than she had before his visit... She had his attention now at least and she anticipated a response from him soon. He hadn't said when he'd be in touch, but she fully believed he would be. The stallion would have to be at the farm when the mares were in season. By her calculations, that should be in the next week or so. They hadn't agreed to any specific terms, but he understood what she wanted from breeding racehorses.

"Lady Katherine," a groom came up to her and spoke. "I don't mean to intrude..."

She stopped brushing Sammy and turned to the man. "What is it?"

"You have a guest," he said. "Would you like me to finish brushing Sammy?

Katherine shook her head. "No, I am done with her." She lifted the brush toward the groom. "Could you see that this is returned to the stable? Leave Sammy here. She'll enjoy some time outside of the paddock."

"Very well, my lady," he said, then took the brush from her. He turned on his heels and left her alone with Sammy.

"Have fun frolicking," she said softly to the

horse. "Sometimes I envy you and the carefree life you have here."

She could probably have a more carefree life herself if she chose to marry and become a boring nobleman's wife. She could plan house parties and balls to entertain the most elite. It would be tedious and dreadful. She liked attending the occasional society function, but for the most part she felt more herself alone on the horse farm. At one time she had envisioned being married to an earl or even a marquess like Lord Holton. She was the daughter of a duke after all. She could have had her pick of the eligible bachelors. Sadly, none of them had really appealed to her. They wanted something from her that she couldn't give them...a biddable wife. Katherine was stubborn, intelligent, and ambitious. Not ambitious like a young lady in search of a husband. Ambitious like a woman determined to be independent and leave the marriage mart to those insipid misses who only wanted a title.

Katherine petted Sammy one last time and then turned to leave her alone in the pasture. She'd be fine in the fenced in grassy area. Katherine was the one reluctant to leave. Sammy probably could care less. She signed and started toward the house. She wasn't sure who her visitor could be but she hoped it was

Lord Holton. He could have written, but he seemed to like having meetings in person. It was more likely for him to make a trip to see her then to send a messenger of any sort.

She reached the house and walked up the steps to the entrance. Her hair was windblown and tiny tendrils had slipped out of the tight chignon she'd had her maid plait up on top her head earlier in the day. Katherine reached up and tucked one strand behind her ear. She probably looked a fright. She took a deep breath and stepped into her sitting room. The house was spacious, but simple. There were 5 bedchambers, a sitting room, a library that also served as her office, a dining room, and a large kitchen. They had an extensive staff for the stables, a housekeeper, a couple maids, and a butler. There were no footman, but a stable hand could act as one in a pinch. It was a modest household that didn't host too many visitors. She didn't know why it suddenly mattered, but it did.

Lord Holton was on the other end of the sitting room staring out the large window on the far side of the room. The sun streamed over his dark brown hair giving the strands golden highlights. He stood straight with his broad shoulders stiff. Did the man ever relax? She took a step forward and spoke, "My apologies for keeping you waiting, my lord."

He turned to face her. His lips tilted upward into an almost devilish smile. "It's I that should apologize. I should have sent word that I'd be arriving today. I had business at one of my estates that kept me away."

"I hope all is well." This politeness between them seemed wrong... "I trust you've made a decision."

"I have," he said. "I will allow you to use Sir Goliath as a stud, but I have some conditions."

Of course he did... "That's wonderful news. What are your conditions?"

"I'd like to stay here while Sir Goliath is in residence and have a full part in the process." He took a step toward her. "Instead of a fee I'd like a stake in the raising of the horses and a fifty percent share in any profits."

He was insane if he thought she'd agree to that. "I find it acceptable for you to remain in residence. I do not agree to the percentage. I'll allow you a fifteen percent share in the profits."

Lord Holton shook his head. "That's much too low. Forty percent."

Katherine gritted her teeth. He wanted too much from her. She needed this to expand her stables and branch out. "Twenty five percent and that is my final offer."

He remained quiet for a few moments and then slowly nodded. "You have a deal," he said. "I've taken the liberty to have the contracts already drawn up." He walked over to a side table and picked up the contracts. "We just need to add in the agreed upon percentage and sign them."

How calculating of him. At least he hadn't assumed she'd agree to his fifty percent demand. She took the contract from him and read it over. If she had learned anything from her absentee father it was to read anything before agreeing to it. She didn't want Lord Holton to spring a surprise or two upon her.

The contract was straightforward. It outlined most of the terms they had discussed when he'd last visited. Sir Goliath would remain at the farm for three months to give him time to breed with the mares. If the mares were to all become impregnated before the three months were finished then he could remove the stallion sooner, but the most Sir Goliath would remain at Katherine's farm would be the agreed upon three month timeframe.

She glanced up at Lord Holton. "If you will follow me we can sign these in the library."

He nodded and then allowed her to lead him to her library. She had a large mahogany desk on the right side of the room near the large windows. The natural light at her back allowed her to work well into the evening if necessary. Sometimes working by candlelight hurt her eyes. She placed the contract on the desk and pulled out her chair. Once seated she picked up a quill and tapped it into her inkpot. She pulled the contract over to her and quickly signed her name to the bottom of the last page. Then she slid the contract back across the desk and held the quill out to Lord Holton. "It's your turn," she said.

He grinned and plucked the quill from her hand, then pushed the tip into the inkpot. He swirled it over the parchment as he pressed the quill against it. His name was a lot of swirls and had more flourish than hers did. It was almost...pretty.

"Now that is done," he began. "I've already ordered my stable master to move the horse here tomorrow. My cousin, Lady Lenora will accompany them. I hope that is all right. It's better for your reputation that we have her here. People will talk if we reside in the house together without the buffer of another lady."

She lifted a brow. "Who would know?" Katherine tilted her head to the side. "And where do you plan on staying tonight? Wouldn't the damage already have been done by the time Lady Lenora arrived?" She really didn't care if Lenora stayed at her farm. She liked the other lady and welcomed the opportunity to become more acquainted with her, but Lord Holton's reasoning made absolutely no sense.

"I'll take lodging in the nearby town," he said. "It's one night I can make do with a bed at the inn. Even if they have a lumpy mattress." He grimaced at the mention of the mattress. He must have stayed at the inn when he last visited the farm.

"Don't be ridiculous," she said. "No one ever visits the farm. Stay here. I trust you to act as a gentleman and even if word did spread of our being alone together it doesn't matter to me. I have no intention of ever marrying."

He lifted a brow. "That's ridiculous. No one would ever do business with you if you were ruined. Your venture will fail before it's even begun."

Lord Holton might be right, but she didn't anticipate that happening. "Suit yourself. If you prefer a lumpy mattress at the inn with subpar food then that is your decision to make." She stood and walked around the desk. "The least I can do is offer you tea before you depart." She lifted a brow. "Or is that too much for you? It might sully your reputation to be alone with me a moment longer."

He pressed his lips together and anger flashed over his eyes. "I'll depart now. Otherwise I fear I may say something I'll come to regret."

"Don't hold back on my account, my lord. I can take any insult you feel the need to throw my way. I'm much stronger than you believe me to be."

Katherine was tired of his high handedness. She didn't need or want his protection. She lifted her chin defiantly awaiting his scathing remarks. He opened and closed his hands at his side. She didn't know why he felt the need to clench them. He'd never hit her. Lord Holton wasn't that sort of man, but the action suggested he was fighting an instinct of some kind.

"You shouldn't taunt me," he said. His breathing was uneven and his cheeks reddened slightly. It was then she realized exactly what he was fighting. He was attracted to her... That was interesting.

"Why not?" She should hold back the retort but she couldn't help herself. The urge to needle him was great and she wanted to see how far she could push him. Would he give in and kiss her? She suddenly wanted his kiss more than anything. She stepped toward him closing the distance between them. "What would you do?"

He stared down at her meeting her gaze. Heat filled her at the intensity of it. Lord Holton lowered his gaze to her lips. She flicked her tongue over them finding them suddenly dry. He didn't move any closer to her, but he seemed to really want to. Lord Holton shook his head, once, then again. For a moment she thought he'd be able to resist the temptation, but then at the last second he reached for her and pressed his lips to hers. She caught fire as his lips rolled over hers. He slipped his tongue into her mouth when she opened it to gasp, taking full advantage of her shock. He ravaged her mouth taking away all thoughts and ability to move. Then suddenly he stopped, wrenched himself away from her and stomped out of the room.

Well... What was she to make of that?

CHAPTER 7

The morning sunlight flowed over Bennett as he rode his horse beside the carriage with his cousin Lenora inside. He'd had a very uncomfortable night in the inn and he was in quite a surly mood. After he'd kissed Lady Katherine he had to put as much distance as he could between them. He still couldn't believe he'd done something so foolish. He'd been so angry with her. Bennett didn't usually want to kiss someone he was that irate with. There was just something about Lady Katherine he found equal parts irresistible and frustrating. He couldn't get her out of his head either. No matter how hard he tried he couldn't stop thinking about her and he wanted to. At least he thought he did.

They reached the long winding path that lead to

the main house on Lady Katherine's horse farm. He rode ahead of the carriage and directly to the stable. He stopped, dismounted, then handed the reins of his horse to a stable hand. "This here is Octavius," he told the groom. "He can be feisty, but he shouldn't be too much trouble."

"We will take good care of him, my lord," the stable hand told him.

Bennett nodded at them and headed toward the house. The carriage had come to stop at the front and the driver was assisting Lenora out. Lady Katherine had come out of the house and stood nearby waiting for Lenora to reach her. He paused a moment and stared at her from the distance. Bennett felt safe viewing her from where he stood. She hadn't even glanced in his direction. Lady Katherine looked lovely as always. She wore a dark blue gown that made her pale skin seem even more beautiful than normal. Her black hair was pulled back, but a few stands escaped and trailed around her neck.

He groaned. What the bloody hell was wrong with him. Bennett wanted to close the distance between them and pull her into his arms. Kiss her again. Over and over until she was breathless... He needed her far more than he liked to admit. He cursed under his breath and forced himself to keep walking toward her. Who was he kidding? She was a flame and he was the bloody moth who couldn't resist her.

When he reached the entrance to the house Lenora was already deep in conversation with Lady Katherine. He stopped by them and nodded at his cousin. "I trust everything is going well."

Lenora shook her head slightly. "Why wouldn't it be?" She tilted her head to the side and stared at him with a puzzled expression.

"I didn't expect anything would be wrong. Just confirming it's..."

"Don't worry, my lord," Katherine interrupted him. "I do know how to act as a hostess."

It seemed as if everything he said to her was wrong. No matter what he did she took it the exact opposite of how he intended it. How was he ever going to get her to be less hostile with him? He wanted so much more that he thought possible with her. Their beginning hadn't been a good one, but he hoped that in the end, they would both be much happier. He believed that they could have something if only he could convince her. "I do not doubt that." He lifted his lips upward into what he hoped was a congenial smile. He'd try to win her over later. If he was lucky she'd be more amenable.

Lady Katherine met his gaze. She stared at him as if she didn't believe he was actually in front of her. It wasn't a good stare either. Her eyes were filled with animosity and if she were capable of it she'd have shot daggers straight at him with just that one look. She glanced away and turned toward Lenora. "If you'll follow me I can show you to your room."

Lenora stepped after her. "Your home is lovely." Bennett followed after them even though Katherine hadn't invited him.

"Thank you," Lady Katherine replied. "I wish I could say it was my decorating skills. I've done little to it since I moved out here a couple months ago."

"I envy you," she said.

"Why?" Katherine asked a little surprised.

"You're so brave. I wish I was..."

Katherine sighed. "One day you'll find your own strength. Until then just be yourself. She patted Lenora's hand "How do you feel about balls and dancing?"

Bennett felt as if he should join the conversation but he was curious why Lady Katherine had bothered to ask Lenora that. Why would she want to know if she liked dancing? Bennett wouldn't mind dancing with Lady Katherine if she would give him the chance.

"I never get asked to dance," Lenora admitted. "I'm a wallflower."

"Well," Katherine began. "That would make a ball tedious."

"Indeed," Lenora agreed. "It's not all bad though. You learn a lot about people when they don't realize you're watching."

That took Bennett by surprise. What exactly had his little cousin observed? When he had a moment alone with her he'd have to ask her a few pointed questions. They moved down the hall past several doors. Finally Lady Katherine stopped at one. "This one is your room. I hope you find it comfortable and if you need anything do not hesitate to ask." She smiled softly. "We have an invitation to dinner and entertainment at Baron Dryden's tonight. If you would rather not go..."

"No," Lenora interrupted her. "I'd like to. It'll be a smaller gathering and I won't be as intimidated by it."

"Good," Lady Katherine said. "I'll let you rest." She turned toward Bennett acknowledging him for the first time since they'd started walking. "This way, my lord."

He fell into step beside her. Bennett wished he

had some inkling what to say to her but he was at a loss for words. "So is this a country ball?"

She shrugged. "Of sorts I suppose."

It wasn't much of an answer. He'd figure out how to get her to open up to him. It would just take a little time. It was doable though. They reached a door and she stopped beside it. She twisted the knob and pushed the door open. "Your room, my lord."

She didn't stop to talk to him as she had with Lenora. He took a deep breath and watched her walk away. He found her incredibly attractive and he might even be falling in love with her.

KATHERINE SAT AT THE VANITY IN HER BEDROOM and finished putting her pearl necklace around her neck. She had on a gown of soft emerald silk. It was not one of her more elaborate gowns, but she loved it all the same. She hadn't expected to attend many balls while residing at the farm. It had come as a bit of a surprise to be invited to one. The spring season would begin in another month and she'd probably go into London to attend some of the larger balls and soirees. An intimate country ball was nice and had a certain appeal to it. As Lady Lenora had mentioned earlier—it was easier.

It was time to go downstairs. She had been doing her best to avoid Lord Holton since he'd moved into her home. If she could have stayed in her bedchamber she would have. At least Lady Lenora made having him around more tolerable.

If only he wasn't so handsome...

He was acting strangely. It had to be because of the kiss. She hadn't asked him to kiss her. Sometimes she wished he hadn't. Other times she wished he would kiss her all over again. She wasn't sure what she wanted anymore and having him around only served to confuse her even more. Katherine had to discern what she truly desired and soon.

She stepped out of her room and descended the stairs. Lady Lenora and Lord Holton were already there waiting for her. "My apologies for keeping you waiting."

"The carriage has already been pulled up for us," Lord Holton announced.

They all went outside and Lord Holton assisted them into the carriage. After they were all securely inside the driver motioned for the horses to move. It didn't take too long to reach the estate of Baron Dryden. Thirty minutes later the carriage was halting in front of the Dryden manor. Lord Holton stepped out before Katherine and Lady Lenora, then reached back in to assist them as they exited the carriage. Katherine took his hand because it would have been rude to refuse his assistance. Tiny sensations shot through her at his touch and she didn't know how to wrap her mind around that. Why was she so drawn toward him? That kiss had changed everything.

"Thank you," Katherine said.

He nodded. "It's my pleasure."

Lord Holton escorted them both inside. Once in the foyer they were greeted by their host Baron Dryden. "Lady Katherine," the baron said. "It's so good of you to join us." He turned his attention to Lord Holton. "I'm glad you and your lovely cousin were able to accompany our new neighbor."

Katherine wanted to sigh but held it in. They all liked having the daughter of the duke as a local. This wasn't the first invitation she had received. There was only one reason she had accepted this one. It gave her some space between her and Lord Holton. She didn't look forward to being alone with him. She had a feeling it would lead no where good.

Lord Holton nodded at Baron Dryden. "It's my pleasure to accompany Lady Katherine to your home. It's been a while since I've had the opportunity to attend any social gathering."

Katherine let Lord Dryden lure the marquess away. She didn't even want to discern the inner workings of either of the lord's minds. Especially Lord Holton. There were times she wished she could understand Lord Holton's motivations, but for one night she just wanted to forget everything. Maybe have a little fun for once. She did feel a little bad abandoning Lady Lenora. She'd make it up to her later.

She walked down the hall and entered the first open door she found. It was a library. She hadn't ever been to Lord Dryden's home and it was probably wrong of her to explore it without permission. Katherine couldn't make herself care though.

"Why are you in here alone?" a male asked.

It startled her a little bit. She turned to find Lord Holton standing in the doorway to the library. "Why are you following me?" she retorted.

"I was worried."

"I'm fine," she told him. "I don't need you to make sure I'm all right." Though a part of her liked the idea he cared enough to seek her out. Did he have some sense when she was out of sorts?

"What if I want to?" He lifted a brow and then

stepped into the room. "I think I may owe you an apology."

She turned and met his gaze. He seemed worried about something. "Whatever for?"

"You've been distant since I returned to the farm with my cousin. I feel I must have offended you..."

He was referring to the kiss. It was the only thing that he probably felt he should apologize for. She laughed a little at that. There was much more that he should feel sorry for. Kissing her wasn't one of them. "Don't worry about what you think you might need to do, my lord."

"But," he started and then shook his head. "What can I do to make things right between us?"

"I don't know," she admitted. "But do not apologize for kissing me. It'll make things much worse between us."

He pressed his lips together into a tight line. He didn't like that answer. Well too bad. It wasn't her responsibility to make him feel better about himself. "I..."

"I think we should return to the baron," Katherine said, not allowing him to finish whatever he hoped to say. She moved past him and walked out of the library and toward the sound of voices echoing through the room.

CHAPTER 8

$\mathcal{D}$inner had gone well. At least Bennett believed it had... It would have been better if he'd been seated next to Lady Katherine, but Baron Dryden had taken that honor. The seating hadn't exactly followed proper etiquette, but complaining wouldn't have benefitted him. He wanted Lady Katherine to look upon him favorably.

They had retired to the sitting room. The men had brandy and the ladies had been served sherry. He found the entire thing tedious. What he really desired was to spend a few moments alone with Lady Katherine, but he couldn't discern a way to make that happen. She was on the far side of the room in a deep conversation with his cousin, Lenora. He wasn't sure that he wanted to know what they could be discussing. His cousin could be... impressionable. He hoped that Lady Katherine wasn't giving her unsavory ideas.

He lifted his glass to his lips and sipped at the brandy. Bennett didn't really want it, but he was also at a lost what to do with himself. They had no entertainment to speak of and he'd been half listening to Baron Dryden for the past half hour droll on about nothing of import. He'd never experience such a sense of ennui before.

"Don't you think so?" Baron Dryden asked.

"Hmm?" He mumbled still distracted by Lady Katherine. He had no idea what Baron Dryden was speaking about and quite frankly he didn't particularly care.

"Dancing," Baron Dryden said. "We have enough to do a few sets, but we'd need someone to play the pianoforte."

"Dancing?" Bennett asked. What a brilliant idea. He could suggest a waltz and pull Lady Katherine onto the floor for a set. She wouldn't be able to escape from him then. He'd have her full attention for several short minutes. "That's a splendid idea. My cousin, Lady Lenora is an excellent musician. We should ask her to play for us."

"Splendid idea," Baron Dryden agreed.

They strolled leisurely over to where Lady Katherine and Lenora were conversing. They stopped their discussion upon their approach. Lady Katherine met his gaze briefly then turned toward the baron. "Baron Dryden we were just discussing what a lovely dinner you hosted for us."

"I'm so glad you've enjoyed it." Lord Baron smiled down at her. Bennett had to stop himself from punching him. He wasn't doing anything untoward. The baron started to speak again focusing his attention on Lenora. "My lady, Lord Holton tells me you're an excellent musician."

"I..I am," Lenora stumbled over the words.

Baron Dryden beamed at her. "Would it be too much to prevail upon you to play for us? It would be wonderful if we had some music to dance with."

Lenora was quiet for a short time. Her face lost all color. His cousin didn't like being noticed and playing might lead some individuals to stare in her general direction. He placed a hand on her arm. "If this is too much for you we understand."

"No," she said and shook her head. "I'll do it..." Lenora swallowed hard and then slowly walked toward the pianoforte.

"May I have your attention." Baron Dryden

raised his voice so everyone could hear. "Lady Lenora St. Martin has generously agreed to play for us so we may have some dancing and entertainment."

The murmurs of approval filled the room. Bennett grimaced a little at their loud appreciation. His cousin nearly shriveled into herself at their attention. He went over to her side and helped her arrange the music. He felt horrible suggesting she play to Baron Dryden. He was a terrible cousin to her. "Are you certain you wish to do this?"

"I can't change my mind now. It's a little too late for that." She sighed. "I need to at least attempt to get past my terror or social situations. This is no way to live."

"I don't wish you to be uncomfortable. Please forgive me. I never should have mentioned to the baron that you're an excellent musician." He'd been selfish when he suggested it.

"You were not lying to him. Don't be hard on yourself," she told him. "This is good for me."

He blew out a breath and glanced past her at Lady Katherine. She was across the room next to the baron, but her attention was on him or rather on Lenora.

"You like her don't you," Lenora said.

"What?" He turned his attention back to her.

"Lady Katherine," she said and gestured in her direction. "I've noticed how you stare at her. Are you thinking of asking for her hand?"

"No," he said immediately. Was he? All Bennett knew for certain was that he'd been drawn to Lady Katherine almost from the start. The problem was that he was clueless on how to handle her. He didn't want to say she wasn't like any other female. That wasn't entirely true. There were lots of females in the world and they all had their similarities and differences. Where Lady Katherine was concerned though, she was different for him. She made his heart beat faster in his chest. He couldn't stop thinking about her. She wasn't afraid to challenge him. Lady Katherine was in some ways...his equal, or at the very least, she demanded to be. That made him want her in ways he never imagined. "I hadn't considered marriage where Lady Katherine is concerned." Why hadn't he? She was a well-connected lady of good breeding. He found her attractive and he enjoyed her company—even when they sparred. She would be a good match for him. So why hadn't he considered marrying her?

"That's a little surprising," Lenora said in a thoughtful tone. "Perhaps you should."

He didn't want to admit aloud that he agreed with her. Bennett still couldn't believe how foolish he'd been acting in regards to Lady Katherine. "I might," he conceded. "Perhaps you'll do me a favor and play a waltz. I'd like to have a few moments of uninterrupted conversation with the lady."

She smiled at him. "Anything for you." She turned toward the music and shuffled through it until she found what she was looking for. "I suggest you make your way to her side so you can claim the first dance. Otherwise Baron Dryden might claim her for himself."

He scowled across the room and headed in their direction. He would not allow the baron to claim what was his. In his mind Lady Katherine was already his wife, and yet, he hadn't considered the possibility until a few moments ago. Now that he had Bennett rather liked the idea. He reached her side and bowed before her. "Lady Katherine I hope you'll do me the honor of leading you in the first waltz."

"There's going to be a waltz?" She beamed. "Oh I do love waltzing. I suppose I can deign to allow you to have the first one."

"My cousin loves playing a waltz," he said

holding back a grin. Truthfully, he didn't know if she did or not. Lenora liked playing anything. His referencing the waltz in particular allowed for her to keep her word to him. In case Baron Dryden had asked for the first dance, she'd have to choose to give Bennett the first one if it was a waltz.

The first strands of the waltz filled the room. She turned toward him and lifted a brow. "I suspect you planned this."

"Does it dissuade you from dancing with me?"

"No," she said after a brief moment. "I keep my word, my lord." Lady Katherine held out her hand to him.

He led her to the small dance floor and swung her into his arms. Then he began to twirl her around the room. This was what he had been wishing for since he had entered the baron's home. Some precious moments where, at the very least, it felt as if it was only him and her in the room. "What is it about waltzing you adore so much?"

She lifted her chin and met his gaze. "It feels as if for the duration of the dance I'm floating on air. Nothing and no one can take the magic away and during that time its as if everything is right in the world. It's perfect and I want to savor it." She had a serene smile on her face. Lady Katherine closed her eyes as if she was immersed in a dream. Her eyelids fluttered open and that wistful expression vanished. "Then it ends and reality returns."

"Is reality so bad?" Bennett truly did want to understand her.

"It is when you're me," she said so softly he almost didn't hear it.

Bennett wanted to take away all her pain. Something told him that she'd been through a great deal. Far more than anyone realized. It had never occurred to him that she acted as she had out of desperation or a need that he couldn't fathom. He'd assumed her motivations were to thumb her nose at society's strictures, but it had to be more than that. Lady Katherine was more complex. She didn't act rashly. Everything she did seemed to come from some carefully crafted plan.

He liked dancing with her. She was a superb dancer and the perfect partner for him. Not once had she stepped on his toes and she followed his lead as if born to do so. He twirled her around the floor and wanted to find a way to take them straight out of the room. Far away from everyone and everything that could interrupt them. She probably wouldn't thank him for it.

"What is your favorite thing to do?" he asked.

"I have many beloved things," she said. "It would take too long to list them all in the time we have left for this dance."

"There isn't one you love above all?" He lifted a brow. "I already know you love dancing. Is there another activity that you enjoy as much?"

"Reading, riding, tea with Diana," she said. "Just to name a few. Diana has the best afternoon tea and the company is always fascinating."

He suspected the Duke of Clare's wife was amongst those guests. He'd heard somewhere that the duchess was Lady Diana's cousin. "Do you have a favorite book?"

"No," she said and shook her head. "It depends on what I feel like reading. Sometimes it is an educational tome and others it is something for pure entertainment. My mood dictates many of my choices."

"So you could decide to read the proper implementation of farming equipment on a whim."

Lady Katherine wrinkled her nose. "That sounds positively dreadful, but there might be some useful information in there. I find I have a lot to learn about estate management. Girls are never taught such things. My father sent me to a finishing school and I was taught how to run a proper household and throw lavish parties. There's much more to life than entertainments."

"Indeed," he felt the need to agree with her. "I've often found life to be more tedious than amusing." The only time he felt anything akin to joy was in her presence.

"That's kind of sad," she said not much above a whisper. Then she met his gaze. "Don't you want more than that? I know I do."

He did. Bennett wanted it with her. He wanted to spend the rest of his days with her by his side, exploring all of life's possibilities. He just had to find a way to convince her of the wisdom of that plan. It would probably take a lot for him to make her see things the way he did. If she wanted to be wooed then he'd do everything he could to win her over.

"I want a great deal of things," he admitted. She just happened to be at the top of that list.

They finished the dance and he led her toward the pianoforte. Lenora had already started into a livelier dance. When they reached Lenora she glanced up and smiled at them and he moved closer to her side, flipping the music pages for her as she rand her fingers across the keys. He owed his cousin and he would do what he could to make sure she found happiness too. She deserved it more than anyone he knew. She'd been through a lot in her short life. Lady Katherine had been claimed for another dance, but he was all right with that. He had time to discern a way to make her his, forever. In the end he would have her as his wife. He refused to accept any other outcome.

atherine walked toward the stables. She had to ride the perimeter and check the fence line. There were stable hands to do it but she wanted to do it herself. She had to find something to do to occupy her mind. She hadn't been able to stop thinking about Lord Holton. He'd been so...nice. They had danced a couple of times. The first dance had opened her eyes and shown her a different side to him. The dance itself was nice and enlightening. That hadn't been what gave her insight to him though. It had been directly after it that made her give him a second glance. He'd been attentive to Lenora and made sure she was comfortable while she played. He had even turned the pages for her when he wasn't dancing.

That was another thing... He had only danced with Katherine. Twice. He'd led her to the floor during the only two waltzes that Lenora had played. When he placed his hand at her waist and held her other in his—tiny sensations erupted throughout her. Her entire body had come alive in ways it never had before. Well, that wasn't entirely true. When he kissed her she'd been all aflutter with emotions she hadn't wanted to think about and her body had tingled long after he left her side.

"Lady Katherine," a stable hand greeted her. "How may I assist you?"

"Have my mount saddled," she ordered.

"Do you require a groom to ride with you?" She probably should but she wanted to be alone. She opened her mouth to tell them no when another male came to stand beside her. Katherine glanced toward him and frowned. Lord Holton had strolled nonchalantly into the stables.

"Prepare my horse as well," he told the stable hand. "I'll accompany Lady Katherine."

She wanted to tell him that she didn't require him to go anywhere with her, but held her tongue. A part of her wanted him to ride with her. She had feelings for him that were confusing her. Having him with her might help her sort them out. So instead of becoming a shrew and ordering him to leave her be she stood quietly next to him. Mainly because she was at a loss for words.

The stable hand brought his horse out first and led him to a mounting block. Lord Holton stepped up and easily slid onto the horses back. Another stable hand led her horse out and assisted her onto its saddle. "Thank you," she said.

She pressed her knee into the horse's side and flicked the reins. The horse started moving. She didn't stop to tell Lord Holton to follow her. Instead she let him figure it out for himself. He was an intelligent male and should be able to discern what to do well enough. Her assumptions about him turned out to be correct. He led his horse forward and fell in step beside her. They rode in silence for several minutes. After they put some distance between them and the house he finally spoke. "Where is it we are going?"

"Nowhere and everywhere, she answered.

"That's rather cryptic." He chuckled lightly. "Do you not wish to share our destination?"

She sighed. "I'm riding the perimeter of my lands and checking for anything that might need addressed. We will look at the fencing and the lands in general. I don't know that we are going to find anything, but I often do find things that need to be repaired when I do these excursions." Not that she'd done them often. She had only been in possession of the property for a short time. This was only the third time she had rode across her land. The first time she'd just wanted to see everything that belonged to her as if she didn't quite believe it.

"Similar to what we did the first time I visited?"

"Sort of," she answered. "I didn't go far that day. We stayed on the east side of the property. We are going to start with the west side and work our way over to the east. Since it wasn't that long ago that I surveyed over there I don't expect to find much in need of repair." She rarely rode on the west side and wasn't as familiar with the land.

They rode in silence until they reach the pasture on the far side of the west. There were two horses grazing inside the fence line. They were mares already pregnant and allowed to graze the lands. It had already started to warm up the frigid temperatures would soon be replaced with spring sunshine. She had three weeks until she returned to London for the season. So she could pretend to be in search of a husband. It was the only way her father would agree to leave her be on her lands. It was his last piece of control he had over her. She wouldn't reach her majority for another year. Until then she would remain under her father's rule.

As they rode along the fence line she glanced up at the sky. Dark clouds had rolled in above them. They were too far from the main house to make it back before the storm rolled in. She cursed under her breath.

"Those are some interesting choice words," Lord Holton commented. "But I have to concur. Where about to be in a bloody mess."

"Follow me, my lord," she ordered. "There is an old cottage up ahead. It needs some repairs but we can take shelter there until the storm passes. There is even a small barn that we can put the horses in."

The barn was meant for pigs or perhaps a couple cows, but it would do for the horses on a short-term basis. She pressed her knee into her horse and motioned for it to gallop toward the cottage. Rain started to fall before they reached the barn. It was light but she was still getting quite wet. They had the horses safely tucked away and then ran toward the cottage. A full down pour erupted on the short trek to the cottage drenching her completely. She didn't stop to look at Lord Holton but assumed he was equally as wet as her.

They bolted inside and he shut the door firmly

behind them. The sky had darkened and there was not much light inside the cottage. "Do you think we can light a fire?" she asked.

"If we have the proper materials it's certainly a possibility." He pointed toward the hearth. "I think I see a tinder box. We just need some wood…"

Lord Holton headed toward the hearth. In a wooden crate there was several logs inside of it. He pulled them out and started working on a fire. Katherine went in search for some candles. There was no way of knowing how long they would be in the cottage. She opened a cedar chest and found a quilt and several unused candles. Katherine pulled out all of it. She set the quilt on a nearby settee and then went in search of a candelabra. She found one on a table and placed the three tapered candles she found in it, then took it over to Lord Holton. "Do you think you can light these?"

He had the fire going and warmth spread over her as she stood near the hearth. Lord Holton lit the candles and handed it back to her. She set it on the table and then went over to the settee. She debated what she should do next. Her dress wasn't as wet as she thought but still considered taking it off to let it dry.

"You found a quilt," he said. "There's only one?"

She glanced at the quilt and then back at him. "We can share it."

"We could," he agreed. "But I don't know what good it would do since we're both so wet." He pulled off his jacket and waistcoat then hung them on a hook. "At least remove your cloak. You're dress won't be as wet as that."

She nodded and did as he suggested. Katherine hung it on a hook near his jacket and waistcoat. Then walked back to the settee. She settled on it and pulled the quilt over her. He sat near her but made no move to share it with her. "You should set your gentlemanly airs aside. It wouldn't do any good for you to catch a chill."

He stared at the quilt for several heartbeats and then glanced back at her. "May I ask you a question?"

"Certainly," she said, but felt uneasy about it. What did he want to know about her?

"Why do you feel so strongly about running the horse farm?"

Katherine blew out a breath. There were a lot of reasons for her desire to keep the farm and make a success of it. "My father is, well, he's a duke."

"I know that," he told her. "But what does that have to do with the farm?"

"My father has strong beliefs about a female's duty. It's why he sent me to a finishing school. He expects me to make a brilliant match and I don't know...give his holdings a boost somehow. This farm is my inheritance from my grandmother and he cannot seize control of it no matter what he does. Even if I marry it will never belong to my husband. It is passed down through the female line of my family. Only a female can truly ever inherit it. So this property is my way of carving out my own place in the world. Something my father can't take away from me and I can do whatever I want with."

"I think I finally understand why you have been so angry with me. I took away something that you needed and chastised you for going to Tattersall's. That's something your father would have done to you isn't it?"

She nodded. "He's quite controlling."

"I'm sorry," he said. "I should never have judged you. I feel like an arse for doing so."

"You wouldn't be the first male to have judged me," she told him. Katherine shrugged. "I should apologize too. You're not the person I thought you to be. For a while there I compared you to my father and it wasn't favorably."

He moved closer and cupped her cheek in his palm. "I want to kiss you again."

Katherine licked her lips. She wanted him to kiss her too, but wasn't so sure it was wise to allow it. "I'd like it if you did."

He leaned down and pressed his lips to hers. That familiar sensation traveled through her. She wanted to move closer to him. Feel his body against hers and let his warmth take control over her. Katherine needed...him. She let the quilt fall to her lap and lifted her arms so they rested around his neck. He pushed his tongue inside of her mouth and she met it with her own. They tasted each other until she couldn't tell where he began and she ended. He pulled back and met her gaze. His breathing was ragged and so was hers.

"I mean to have you," he said.

"What?" The word came out breathy. "How do you mean to have me?" Did he mean marriage or in the carnal sense. Perhaps he meant both...

"In every way possible," Lord Holton admitted. "I want you more than I've ever desired anything."

God she wanted him to. She loved him. How had she failed to realize that before this moment. All their arguing was leading to this moment. They had to find their way to each other. Katherine wasn't sure he loved her in return though. "Lord Holton..."

"Bennett," he said. His eyes blazed with desire and his voice was hoarse as he spoke.

"Pardon me?" She lifted a brow. What was he trying to tell her?

"Call me Bennett," he told her. "We're going to spend the rest of our lives together. I think we should be allowed to use each other's first names."

She shook her head. "I don't recall agreeing to any of those terms." She still wasn't certain what he was asking of her. He had to be clearer because it seemed as if her head was filled with clouds and air. She couldn't think straight no matter how hard she tried.

"Katherine," he began. "My love. The only woman who could ever steal my heart. Will you do me the honor of becoming my wife and spending the rest of our days together?"

Marriage. He definitely meant marriage. That was... Her heart burst into rapid heartbeats. They thundered in her ears and she couldn't make out any of the sounds around her. He wanted her to be his wife. He loved her... Katherine brought both of her hands up to his face. When the day started out as it had she never would have imagined it would lead to this moment. That he would openly admit he loved her.

"On one condition," she said. Marriage was final and she had to make sure that this man would honor her in all ways. She hated to do it, but she had to test him. See just how committed he was to her. If he really loved her... She didn't finish that thought. Katherine opened her mouth and waited breathlessly for him to respond.

"Anything," he told her.

"Sir Goliath will remain on the farm and help me build my race horse stock," she said. He had been so against her having the stallion. It really was the only test she could give him to see how far he'd go to please her.

"Are you only agreeing to marry me for my horse?" He raised a brow. "That's..." He chuckled softly and shook his head. "I will concede to that if you allow him to race in the spring meet. Then he can retire to the farm." He plucked one of her hands from his cheek and pressed a kiss to her palm. "Now tell me you love me and you'll be my wife."

"I do and I will," she said. "But I don't want a large wedding. I'd rather race off to Scotland and skip the contracts my father will demand. Let's go and not give him a reason to interfere." He truly did

DAWN BROWER

love her. Bennett was not asking too much in return for giving her the stallion. Truthfully, she was being greedy for demanding he give Sir Goliath to her. She'd agree to allow him to race the horse more than just the spring race, but they could discuss that later.

"I don't think we need to do anything that drastic," he said. "I'm a wealthy lord of the realm. I surely can afford the proper bribes to the Arch Bishop and obtain a special license."

Katherine grinned. She loved him so much. "You're the perfect man for me and I cannot wait until we are married. I have a feeling we will have the most interesting of lives together."

"You can count on it," he told her and then leaned down to kiss her again.

What were the odds she'd find love with the Marquess of Holton? Katherine would never have bet on them falling madly, deeply for each other. Sometimes fate had a way of bringing two unlikely individuals together. It certainly had worked its magic on them. It had started with her scandalous visit at Tattersall's and not long after it had grown into a love for the ages. It wasn't often that scandal had a chance to meet love so perfectly. Katherine thanked her lucky stars it had for her...

EPILOGUE

May 1816

The sun was high in the sky and its rays draped them in warmth. Katherine tilted her face upward to fully appreciate the heat. She had her eyes closed as if caught in a daydream. They were at the spring race awaiting Sir Goliath's entry into England's racing world. She had faith he'd come through and win. Everything else in her life had gone better than she could have planned. Why not this too? If Sir Goliath won the foals they expected from Katherine's breeding program would be worth so much more.

"Are you happy?" Bennett leaned down and brushed a kiss against her cheek.

She didn't open her eyes. Katherine savored the feel of his lips against her skin. How was she to express how happy she was? They'd been married two months and it still felt surreal to her. She had never fully believed she'd find love. Some how luck had been on her side and led her to the one man guaranteed to steal her heart. She let her eyelids flutter open and she turned to meet his gaze. "More happy than I could ever express."

He pressed his lips to hers in a soft sweet kiss. Bennett lifted his head and asked, "Want to make a wager?"

Katherine chuckled lightly. "Oh, I already have."

He lifted a brow. "With who?"

She nodded in the direction of the Duke and Duchess of Blackmore. "Narissa and I have a side bet. She is actually betting against Sir Goliath. Can you believe that? She insists he's too green to win on his first run."

Bennett closed his eyes and took a deep breath. He opened them and said, "She may be right."

"Don't you lose faith now," she chastised him. "Our horse will win."

"What is the wager?"

Katherine twisted her lips into a wanton smile.

"If Narissa should win," she began. "She gets her pick of Sir Goliath's foals."

"I thought she already had that..." He tilted his head in confusion.

"She won't have to pay for it," Katherine clarified. "She gets to train it as she sees fit and race it if she chooses to. However, if she does race it we still will get a percentage of its winnings."

Bennett sighed. "And if Sir Goliath should win?"

She loved him. He didn't admonish her for making the wager. No, her husband wouldn't make that mistake with her. He accepted her—faults and all. Every day she adored him more than the last. Her heart was so full it was brimming with love. "I get a stake in Lady Fortuna's. Not just the racing part that I'll bring in, but the entire overhead. It's not much—a mere two percent, but it'll be worth it."

Fortuna's Parlor was Narissa's project. The one that helped her achieve her goals. It was also the thing that had brought them all together. Her closest friends were a part of the gaming hell in some way. They each had their own scandalous behavior and thus far, it had led them to the love of their lives. No men were allowed in the club. Their husbands would still sneak in from time to time though.

He kissed her forehead. "I hope you win, but either way know I love you and I always will."

"That's all I need," she answered. "I love you too."

They sat back in the open carriage near the racetrack. It was more peaceful than braving the stands. There were too many people and Katherine abhorred crowds. The jockey riding Sir Goliath led him to the starting gate. A gunshot went off and the horses erupted forward. The race didn't take long but it felt as if it took forever. Her heart beat heavily in her chest.

Sir Goliath was four horses behind. They still had half the track to go. The jockey smacked him several times and he launched forward. The stallion passed one horse, then another, until he was in second place. "Come on, Sir Goliath," she yelled. They were almost to the finish line. She had to win. She just had to...

At the last second Sir Goliath pulled forward and then...he was over the finish line in first, by a nose. He'd won. She jumped up in the carriage hopping around like a child who'd just been given her first pony. Katherine couldn't recall the last time she'd been this happy. No, that wasn't true. She'd been far happier on her wedding day.

Bennett pulled her back into his lap and kissed her until she forgot about the race, the wager, and the world around her. This was what mattered most. The love she'd found against all odds. The rest was just added benefits that she'd appreciate when she could. Bennett, however, would always be the one person she would love until the end of her days.

EXCERPT: BELIEVE IN LOVE

SCANDAL MEETS LOVE 5

AMANDA MARIEL

Believe in Love

USA TODAY BESTSELLING AUTHOR
Amanda Mariel

Cumbria, England, 1804

Lady Brooke Linwood frolicked through a fragrant field of lavender; her skirts held high in her hands. The sun warmed her face while a soft summer breeze kept her from overheating. She inhaled a deep breath of summer, then smiled at her grandparents neighbor, Drake Kingston, The Marquess of Grafton.

"Don't be shy," she called across the open space as she twirled. "Come dance with me."

Drake grinned as he strolled toward her, his black hair bouncing in the breeze and green eyes sparkling. "I've never been shy." He held his arms wide, inviting her to him.

Brooke laughed as she raced into his embrace. She tipped her head back as he twirled her about before bringing her back to him.

Things between them were always this way, fun and easy. Drake made her laugh every time they were together. Provided her an escape from her loneliness. How Brooke wished she could stay here forever.

Alas, she could not. Her Mother had dumped her at her grandparent's estate for the summer. Neither she nor Father could ever be bothered with Brooke. They were far too busy enjoying their separate lives. Brooke was nothing more than an inconvenient daughter.

Soon, Brooke would be sent away to finishing school at Mrs. Emmeline's School of Education and Decorum for Ladies of Outstanding Quality in Canterbury. She wasn't even returning home beforehand. One more way for her parents to ignore her and the knowledge stung.

Not that she cared overmuch about home, but Canterbury... It might as well be a world away from Cumbria and more importantly, Drake. Brooke leaned into him, her heart heavy with the longing. She nuzzled against his shoulder. "I wish I could stay here forever. I'm going to miss you. Miss this."

"Really?" Drake asked as he grinned down at her. "Don't you want to see what else is out there? Aren't you at least a little excited about school?" He arched a brow. "I'll miss you, but I won't forget you."

Brooke sighed, her heart pounding. "We're only fourteen and fifteen. You'll forget about me long before we are grown, and I don't care what's out there. I'm happy here."

"I promise you will find happiness elsewhere. There will be lots of girls at school, and you will make more friends." Drake lifted her from her feet and twirled her in circles. He smiled as he spun her faster, her laughter bursting forth. "That's my girl."

Brooke's heart filled too bursting. For the thousandth time this summer, she wondered if she might love him. It was an emotion she had no experience in other than knowing what love wasn't.

It certainly wasn't parents who did everything possible to avoid their daughter. It wasn't loneliness and tears. Love couldn't possibly be people who cared more for themselves than anyone else.

Love had to be something more, something like this. She tipped her head back, letting the sun warm her face as the surrounding blue sky and lavender swirled past. Her heart swelled as she met Drake's gaze.

Perhaps love was laughter and lighthearted fun? Maybe, just maybe, it was people who enjoyed each others company? A boy and a girl who listened to each other and genuinely cared what they felt. A fluttering belly and excitement when they saw each other.

Did Drake's belly flutter as hers did? He certainly smiled when she came near. And he always made time for her.

"You look like a great bird with your gown flying out around you and head tipped back," Drake said. "A beautiful swan."

"I do not." Brooke laughed harder as he spun her in an up and down pattern as though she truly were in flight.

He set her back on her feet and grinned mischievously. "Laughter looks good on you."

"Then, I shall endeavor to do it more often." Brooke turned and strolled several feet away before glancing over her shoulder to issue a challenge. "Catch me if you can."

"I'll capture you before you reach the ridge." Drake burst into a full run.

"Never." She raced away, leaving a trail of laughter in her wake. The lavender rubbed against her ankles and calves while she ran across the ground.

"Got you," Drake called out a moment before his arm came around her.

Brooke's knees buckled, and they both tumbled to the warm earth. She giggled as she stretched out to gaze up at the puffs of white trailing across the sky. Drake stretched out beside her, his head even with hers and body pointing in the opposite direction. They were like two spokes on a carriage wheel joining in the middle.

She closed her eyes and sighed. "If you were a bird, where would you fly?"

"Everywhere," Drake said. "How about you?"

Brooke thought for a moment not at all sure how to answer for she was already where she wanted to be. She turned her head to gaze at Drake. "I would follow you."

He turned his face to meet her gaze and grinned. "We would have the best adventures. I'd lead you all over the world, and we would see all the places people talk and write about. It would be such fun."

Brooke sat up and pulled her legs to her chest, hugging her knees. "Too bad we are not birds."

"Right," Drake said. He put his hands behind his

head and crossed his ankles. "Still though, we could travel together someday."

"Yes," Brooke said, though in her heart she knew they would not. Drake would grow up and meet some other lady. He'd marry, and travel, and have a family, and she would be a long-ago memory if he remembered her at all.

Drake rolled onto his side and propped his head upon one of his hands. "Let's plan on it. Once we are grown, I will find you. England isn't that big, and I'm to be a powerful duke."

Brooke wanted to point out how unlikely it was that he would even want to come for her, but instead, she decided to play along. What would it hurt to indulge in a little fantasy? She smiled at him, her depression easing. "Then. We will run off and see the world together."

"Indeed. We'll start on the continent then when we've grown board, we will book passage elsewhere." Drake tapped his fingers on the ground. "Where would you like to go?"

Brooke closed her eyes and imagined them traveling to points near and far. "Paris, to start, and then Egypt."

Drake reached for her hand and gave a little squeeze. "Then Paris will be our first destination. I'll take you all around the city. We'll see all the sights and eat all the French food we can stand. You will shop at the most exclusive boutiques and buy the latest fashions before we depart for Egypt."

"That sounds like great fun." Brooke returned his squeeze, wrapping her small hand around his long fingers and wide palm. "We can visit museums, and you can explore the clubs and gaming hells and go hunting. Do all of the things a gentleman explorer does."

Drake grinned at her, his grass-green eyes full of excitement as he sat up. "We will do it all together. I want you at my side for everything, Brooke. I want it to be then, just as it is now."

"Me too," Brooke said, meaning it with her whole heart. "More than you know."

Drake brought his hand to the side of her face, resting it on her cheek. "I'm going to kiss you."

Before she could say anything, he pressed his lips to hers. A gentle touch of flesh upon flesh that sent her heart into a flurry and her head swimming. Her first taste of intimacy. Her first kiss.

A moment that would make their parting all the harder, but also a memory she would cherish always.

CHAPTER 1

London, England, 1814

A crush of people filled Bond Street as Brooke stepped out of the modest shop. Her long-time friends Narissa, the Duchess of Blackmore, and Hannah, the Marchioness of Ramsbury, followed her onto the sidewalk while their footmen carried their packages.

Narissa was expecting her first child and as such was determined to mix with polite society. Her goal was to be respectable by the time she started to show. To that end, Brooke and Hannah came along with Narissa to purchase gowns and fripperies for the ball Narissa and her husband Seth were hosting.

"I do hope we have a good turn out," Narissa said.

Brooke glanced at Narissa and shook her head. "You fret too much." She smiled at her friend. "You are a duchess. The *ton* will come in droves just to say they were at the Duke and Duchess of Blackmore's ball."

"She's right, you know," Hannah added. "You always have a good turn out."

Narissa sighed and patted her belly. "Getting them to come is easy. It's getting them to view us as respectable that I'm worried about. I want this baby to be accepted in society."

"Come now." Brooke waved her hand in front of her chest. "You have never cared about what society thinks. Don't make yourself sick over it now."

"Of course you are right, but for my child, I'll bow down to every matron of the *ton*." Narissa brushed a stray lock of hair from her cheek. "Seth and I plan to win them over, no matter the cost."

"Then, you shall." Hannah smiled.

Brooke stepped around a cluster of children skipping rocks across the sidewalk. Two boys and a girl that looked to be around six or seven years of age. All three were dressed in faded clothing and had dirt streaking their faces. Nonetheless, they were jubilant as they played.

She paused and reached into her reticule to pluck out a few coins. Extending her hand to the children, she said, "Take these and get yourselves a treat."

The little girls' eyes grew wide at the sight of the coins while one of the boys scooped them out of Brooke's hand. "Thank you, my lady," the third child said.

Brooke smiled then pivoted to go. She took a step with her attention still on the children and collided into a hard mass. "Oh!" Brooke lost her footing and stumbled. What a cake she was, walking around with no mind for her surroundings. Now she'd collided with another person. Her cheeks burned.

The strangers' arms came around her, steadying her. "I've got you."

"Thank you." Her breath caught as her gaze collided with familiar green eyes. Eyes she'd not gazed upon in years. "Drake...Your Grace," she quickly corrected for they were no longer children, and using his given name was more than a bit scandalous.

He released her and stepped back, offering a bow. "Lady Brooke. It's been a very long time."

"Yes," her voice cracked, "Too long."

Hannah nudged Brooke with her elbow.

Brooke could scarcely look away from Drake. Her heart was pounding, a million long ago thoughts and emotions racing through her.

He smiled, then glanced from Brooke to Hannah and back again. "Are you going to—"

"Yes, sorry," Brooke said, her cheeks heating. "Allow me to introduce you to my dearest friends, Lady Hannah," she nodded to Hannah," and "Her Grace, the Duchess of Blackmore," she indicated Narissa.

"It's a real pleasure to meet you both." Drake gave another bow. "I am the Duke of Grafton."

"Your Grace," Hannah and Narissa said in unison as they curtsied.

Narissa glanced around at the crush of people scurrying up and down Bond Street, many of them stepping aside to move around the group. "It seems we are impeding travel. Perhaps we should be on our way?"

Brooke stared into Drake's warm eyes, not at all ready to leave him. She had a million questions, a lifetime of curiosity.

"How rude of me." Drake smoothed his cravat. "You ladies are obviously busy." He averted his attention to their nearby footman. "I'll let you continue on with your shopping."

"Actually we are finished." Hannah smiled. "But we should be on our way all the same."

Narissa hooked her hand through Brooke's elbow and gave a little tug.

"Indeed," Brooke said, her gaze locked on Drake's, "it was nice to see you again, Your Grace."

"Likewise, though I'd like to spend more time with you." He gave a wide grin. "May I call on you tomorrow?"

"I'd like that," Brooke said.

Drake's grin brightened. "Until then, my lady."

Brooke gave a slight curtsy before Narissa fairly dragged her down the street to their waiting carriage. She could scarcely believe she'd just come upon Drake—about knocked him off his feet and made a ninny of herself in the process. Lord, what must he think?

Did it even signify?

She shook her head as she stepped into the carriage. Of course not. How could anything matter after all this time? It could not. Whatever might have been between her and Drake was in the past. Brooke released a breath as she smoothed a wrinkle from her skirt.

Narissa settled beside Brooke, and Hannah took the leather bench seat across from them. No sooner did the carriage jerk into motion than Hannah turned a wide grin on Brooke. "Tell us all about him?"

"Who?" Brooke asked. She knew perfectly well who Hannah was inquiring about but could not help but tease her friend.

"The duke, of course." Hannah leaned forward, her eyes sparkling with curiosity.

Narissa angled her body toward Brooke. "I cannot recall you ever mentioning the Duke of Grafton before. How do you know him?"

Brooke loosened the ties of her bonnet, then removed it and placed it on her lap. "He wasn't a duke when I knew him. It's been ten years since I last saw Drake. Ahem," she cleared her throat, "that is since I last saw His Grace."

"You must have been close since you keep using his given name rather than his title," Hannah said.

Brooke's cheeks warmed as she silently chastised herself. She would have to watch her tongue more closely. It simply would not do to run about calling a duke by anything other than his honorary address.

Narissa patted Brooke's hand. "And the way he

seemed to render you speechless lends itself to him being more than a passing acquaintance."

"Nonsense," Brooke rolled her eyes, "He is an old childhood friend. I haven't seen him in ten years and never expected that I'd literally run into him on Bond Street." She smiled as she relaxed against the carriage seat with feigned nonchalance. "I'm quite recovered now."

"Very well," Narissa said. "Though I might add that he seemed quite taken with you."

"Shocked is more like it," Brooke said.

"I imagine so." Hannah laughed.

Brooke turned her attention to the window and gazed out at the passing horses and carriages. A small part of her wondered if Drake had come back for her, but after all this time, she doubted it. No, he was in London for something else entirely, and she'd do best to remember that.

After all, he'd been a duke for several years now. Brooke made a habit of searching for his name in the gossip columns, and on the rare occasions she heard someone speak of him, or his family, she paid close attention. If Drake wanted her, he would have found her sooner.

Nonetheless, Brooke was curious as to why he'd

come to London. She'd be sure to discover his motivation tomorrow.

Her heart fluttered at the knowledge that she'd soon see Drake again and she sighed. Traitorous organ. She'd have to be careful not to give herself over to fanciful ideas where Drake was concerned.

EXCERPT: CHANCE OF LOVE

SCANDAL MEETS LOVE 6

DAWN BROWER

Chance of Love

USA TODAY BESTSELLING AUTHOR

Dawn Brower

PROLOGUE

April 1816

Spring had always been her favorite season. Lady Lenora St. Martin didn't have much else to look forward to and the very idea of new beginnings appealed to her. Every spring new life sprouted and the barren landscape was filled with beauty and wonder. That also applied to the London ballrooms. New debutantes were launched in society and the latest crop of true English beauties was put on display for those gentlemen in search of a wife.

Lenora had never been considered a beauty...

She'd accepted her lot in life a long time ago. She

had dark brown hair and hazel eyes, both boring. Her attributes along with her shyness kept her position as a wallflower secure. No one noticed her and most of the time that was all right with her. A crowded ballroom tended to bring out her worst anxieties. Her cousin Bennett, the Marquess of Holton, insisted she attend social gatherings. Lenora understood his reasons even if she didn't particularly agree with them. Bennett hoped she'd find a suitor, fall in love, and then marry so she could have a family of her own. All of those things sounded wonderful. None of them were likely to happen. At least not with her...

This ball, the one most debutantes and their mothers clamored to attend, was a good example. The young misses were all flirting with their gentlemen suitors and their mothers gossiped with other matrons. The wallflowers did what they did best—hugged the walls. Lenora; on the other hand, did none of that. She didn't merely stand by the wall hoping some wayward gentleman would discover her and lead her to the dance floor. That would have been too simple and probably preferred by her cousin. No, Lenora didn't do anything by normal standards. She hated to be noticed and would have loved to have remained at home reading one of her favorite novels. So she attempted to make the best of a terrible situation and hid in the darkest most obscure corner she could find.

Spring might mean new beginnings, but it also meant new social gatherings. It led to her greatest discomfort and she dreaded it. If she'd been left alone to walk in the gardens or bask in the warmth of sunlight streaming through her bedroom window she'd have been gloriously happy. Instead she was forced into ballrooms and hiding in corners.

"What's a lovely woman such as yourself doing in this dark corner?" His voice was as warm as honey on a hot summer day. It's tempting sweetness washed over her and made her crave a taste...of something. He was also the biggest rake in all of London. Julian Everleigh, the Duke of Ashley was a notorious seducer. "Come dance with me little mouse."

Lenora wrinkled her nose at his endearment for her. She adored Julian, but she knew better than to accept anything he offered. He visited her cousin often enough she should be unaffected by his flirtations. They thrilled her though and she wanted to savor them whenever he deigned to speak to her. "No thank you," she said softly. "I'm all right, promise."

He chuckled lightly and then tilted his lips upward into the most sinful smile she'd ever witnessed. Not that she'd seen many... Most gentlemen failed to notice her let alone smile purposely in her direction. "You shouldn't promise something that isn't true little one," he said. "I don't ever bother with a promise because I know myself too well. I'll break them the first chance presented to me." Julian winked at her and it sent flutters through her stomach she'd never felt before in her entire life. "Instead I'll ensure you will never forget dancing with me. I'm quite good at it." He held out his hand. "Now please, do me the honor of spending a few moments with me. I'm in desperate need of protection from unwanted advances." He leaned down just enough so that she could feel his warm breath when he spoke. "Are you willing to be my savior?"

In that moment she'd have promised him anything, but she held back. He said promises were nothing to him. The duke openly admitted to breaking them often. The vow she was about to make would be empty words to him. So instead she smiled, even if it was a little wobbly. Dancing in front of everyone terrified her. "I can try..."

"That's all anyone can ask," he told her.

Why did he have to be so gorgeous? He was too handsome and way too pretty to be paying any attention to her. His golden blond hair rivaled the sun in brilliance and his blue eyes were more dazzling than the most exquisite sapphire. She could easily become lost in his charming veneer if she allowed herself to be. "I supp..suppose," she stuttered over the word. Lenora cleared her throat and began again. "I suppose that is true."

"So?" He lifted a brow. "Will you join me for the next set?"

She nodded as the strands of a waltz filled the room. Lenora almost groaned when she realized what she'd agreed to. The waltz was the most intimate dances and she'd never danced one with a male other than her cousin. Heck, she'd never danced at all with a male besides her cousin... That didn't detract from her dilemma. A waltz with the duke would cause a stir and she'd be so close to him... Her hand shook as she placed it in his. "Lead the way, Your Grace."

He led her to the floor and then he twirled her into the dance before she had time to change her mind, and she'd been close to doing so. The closer she'd stepped toward the light and the prying gazes of the ton she'd become increasingly more anxious. He'd been wise to take the decision away from her.

Julian was an amazing dancer, but that shouldn't have surprised her. Everything about him or that he did seemed to be perfect. "Now," he began. "This doesn't seem so bad does it, little one?"

At least he hadn't called her a mouse again... "No," she agreed. It was actually quite exhilarating. Lenora felt as if she was floating on air.

"I've always considered dancing to be too decadent to be done properly in a public forum," he began. "At least the sort I prefer."

She pushed her eyebrows together. "I'm not sure I follow..."

"I wouldn't expect you would," he replied secretively. "One day you might understand. Perhaps you'll tell me when you do." The corner of his lip turned upward almost...arrogantly. As if only he really understood the secrets of the world...

"I suspect, Your Grace, that our paths won't cross much in the coming years." The duke might be one of her cousin's friends, but she fully expected, at some juncture, to live on her own. Once she reached her majoring in a few months she planned to travel. Maybe to Italy... She hadn't fully decided yet. "We don't keep the same company and in time the little connections we have will dissipate."

"Perhaps," he agreed. "Time will tell I suppose." He twirled her around the floor expertly.

Lenora wouldn't ever forget this moment. She would unlikely never dance again, at least not like this. She was grateful she'd allowed the duke to convince her to participate. Afterward she'd likely find her way to her favorite corner to hide. In her darkest moments she'd be able to travel back to this waltz and recall it, and Julian fondly. If she believed she had a chance of something more with him... She shook that thought away. Loving him was a terrible idea and perhaps the only thing she regretted. This was a kindness, while out of character for him, but she shouldn't expect anything else from him.

The strands of the waltz ended and disappointment filled her. She'd tried to brush his request off at the start and now she never wanted the dance to end. The duke twirled her one last time around the floor and then led her to where their dance had begun. He bowed and kissed her gloved hand. "Thank you for your benevolence, my lady." His blue eyes twinkled with mischief. "And for being my protector when I need it."

She should be thanking him. He had awakened

feelings in her she'd believed long buried. Her heart burst with happiness and affection for this man. "You don't require my protection any more than you needed to dance with me." She frowned. Lenora still couldn't discern his motives for insisting on leading her in the waltz. "Either way the dance was lovely. I'm grateful I didn't insist against it."

He laughed lightly and shook his head. "Little mouse you're always so formal." Julian bowed again. "The pleasure was all mine." He glanced over his shoulder and then back at her. "Pardon me," he said. "I must attend to something important." His smile was bright and appeared genuine. "Enjoy the rest of your evening, my lady." With those words he spun on his heels and headed in the opposite direction.

Lenora smiled as she watched him wander off. She was starting to believe she had misjudged him. He'd been charming, as expected, but also kind and generous with his time. The duke hadn't been required to dance with her. No gentleman was. That made his attention all the more precious to her.

She wandered away from her favorite corner for willingly the first time all evening. Earlier didn't count because Julian had to coax her away from it. Perhaps she should leave the ballroom and explore the gardens. It was starting to become suffocating in the ballroom. Lenora's happiness was nearly bursting from within her. She hugged herself and twirled around as she made her way down the empty hallway leading to the balcony. There was a small staircase on the balcony that led down to the gardens.

Voices echoed back to her. Two male voices to be more precise and both were recognizable.

"Did she dance?" Her cousin asked. Why was Bennett so concerned about her dancing? Why couldn't he leave her to make her own decisions?

"Of course she did," Julian responded. "Do you doubt my ability to charm a woman?" He sounded so...disgusted. Was that because he had to dance with Lenora or because Bennett had doubted his ability? "I can coax any woman to do, well, anything," he boasted. "But a wallflower? That's not even a challenge."

She'd been jubilant until that moment. Now every amount of joy she'd held inside of her deflated in an instant. He'd appeared so kind earlier... How had she gotten it so wrong?

"Attention from you should have caught the notice of all the eligible gentleman in the room," Bennett said. "They'll want to know why the Duke of Ashley bothered with a wallflower. Soon she'll have more callers than she wants."

She didn't want any callers... A part of her hated her cousin for insinuating himself into her life this way. Why did he ask his friend to pay attention to her? Did he hate having her live with him that much? She'd thought they were closer than that...

"I've done you this favor," the duke said. "Don't ask it of me ever again." His tone was harsh and unyielding. It stabbed her in her fragile heart. She'd been on the brink of falling in love with him. The Duke of Ashley didn't deserve her affection. Lenora doubted he was worthy of any woman's love.

Tears stung her eyes and slid down her cheek. She brushed them away with a swipe of her fingertips. They wouldn't help her and they were as useless as her ability to read people. Lenora hardened her heart in that moment. She'd never play the fool again. It was time she learned to weave her way through society without letting another touch her soul again. She'd never be so easily duped again, but she had a lot to learn. There was one person who could teach her and she'd do whatever it took to convince her. That one person was the new Lulia Prescott—the gypsy Duchess of Clare...

With her decision made she rushed out of the

ballroom and walked all the way to the Holton townhouse. She'd need a good night of rest before she started her journey. Her first stop would be Tenby, Wales to visit with the duchess. After that she'd travel as planned. When she returned to London again she'd be an entirely different, better woman.

EXCERPT: A TREASURED LILY

A MARSDEN ROMANCE

DAWN BROWER

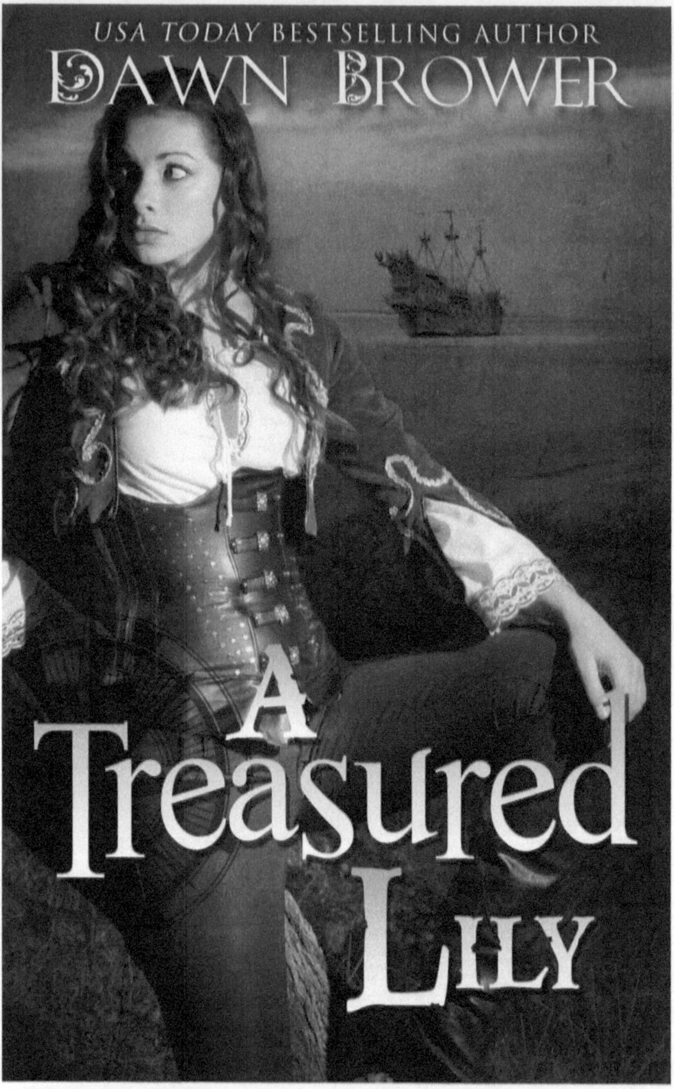
USA TODAY BESTSELLING AUTHOR
DAWN BROWER
A
Treasured
Lily

"*I* just don't think it's a good idea."

"Nonsense." Lilliana Marsden looked up at her best friend, Lady Gemma Kemsley, and frowned. "It's a brilliant idea. My father is being unreasonable about allowing me to travel to America. The plantation in South Carolina is my inheritance. It's about time I claimed it."

"It's not going to work for you to just show up and claim it though. I don't get why you are in such a hurry. You know full well you won't inherit it until you marry." Gemma reached up and smoothed over her sanguine curls, tucking a loose strand behind her ear.

"Well, that's not entirely true." Lilliana's lips twitched into a cheeky smile; it helped to have a little

149

insight into how her parents worked. Gemma didn't know how much she'd gotten away with over the years. Eavesdropping had become a habit of hers. A person could find out the most interesting things quite by accident. When she overheard her parent's most recent conversation she couldn't help the glee that filled her soul. Reining in her excitement had taken an enormous amount of restraint. She needed to leave England and start the life she envisioned for herself. One she had complete control over. Her parent's still hoped she would settle down and get married, but they didn't know her true reasons. "I stumbled across a bit of information that may help me to achieve my goal."

"I don't understand. Did you find a way to inherit it early?"

Lilliana got up, walked to the window of the sitting room, and pulled open the curtains. She stared out at the garden and pondered how to explain what she overheard, and exactly how it fit into her idea to get everything she wanted. Various shades of roses, red, orange, and white, scattered across the garden in a pattern that reminded Lilliana of a kaleidoscope. The garden remained one of the places that she turned to when she needed to reflect on what floated through her mind. It calmed her and made it possible for her to think rationally about any issue that arose in her life. Something about being surrounded by the plant life helped her to think and form her plans with a clear head. Lilliana needed to get Gemma to aid her in her quest to leave England. They worked their magic on her as she calmly let the curtain go and turned back towards her best friend.

"I don't *ever* plan on getting married. I told you that the day we met. My parents still insisted on a season or two. They believe everyone is capable of finding love. They don't understand they are a rarity."

A sting of pain stabbed through her heart, Lilliana rubbed her chest in an attempt to erase the phantom ache. After her disastrous first season, she knew quite well how unusual it was for a love match to exist within the ton. Her choices were lecherous old men and scheming vermin only after her money. There was one man though who made her want to believe he really loved her. She found out the hard way he only wanted to use her. She was thankful he didn't achieve his goal and Lilliana came out relatively unscathed, but the damage to her belief in love sat firmly in place.

"Most matches are made for business or political

reasons. It's all about money and there is no way I'm handing over mine to a male to control."

Gemma tilted her head and crinkled her nose in confusion. Lilliana knew she didn't get it. Her friend wanted to get married and have children. The two years difference in their ages showed when they discussed the possibility of matrimony. In time, Lilliana believed Gemma would look back on this conversation with clarity. In the midst of starting her first season and barely seventeen years old, Gemma still approached life with rose-colored glasses on. For a brief moment in time Lilliana had worn that same veil of hope; her parent's love inspired her enough to want to find it herself.

Reality came crashing in like a bolt of lightning and shattered every ounce of optimism she held within her. Lilliana realized finding love at the various parties hosted within London society equaled finding a mythical creature. The chances of finding a unicorn would be an easier feat. So she gave up on love and formed a new plan for her life.

"I still think you are being preposterous. Why are you so against marriage?" Gemma folded her arms across her chest and stared at Lilliana. Her eyes pinning her in place as she spoke. "That's what a lady is expected to do after all. I just don't understand how you plan on claiming your inheritance without the benefit of a husband to help you get it."

Lilliana could feel her lips twitch into a smile. Her mother often commented on how Lilliana received all her father's traits, even his less than desirable ones. William Thorston Marsden, fifth Viscount Torrington, had a way of getting what he wanted out of people. She admired that characteristic in her father and sought to emulate it. Still, she wished she had been lucky enough to get her mother's pale blonde hair instead of her father's dark curls. In Lilliana's mind, her twin brother, Liam, was blessed because he inherited her mother's coloring.

"I suppose I should explain it so you won't be left in the dark. I'll need your assistance after all."

Gemma got up from her seat and crossed to the window where Lilliana still stood. "You're my best friend. I'll help if I can, but I'm going to be honest and say I don't like this. I don't want to lose you. Please reconsider."

"I will miss you, but I need to find my own way. Please understand this is the best thing for me."

Gemma sighed and then pulled Lilliana into her arms for a hug. Lilliana wrapped her arms around her best friend. She had been curious about Gemma once she realized who she was. Lady Gemma Kemsley had been the girl her father wanted her brother to marry when they were younger. She sought out an introduction to get her measure and hadn't been disappointed in the young woman. They had only been friends for a few months, but in all her nineteen years she had never been close to another female her age. It didn't matter that a couple years separated their age; they were a different kind of soul mate. They appreciated each other on a level that no one else ever could or would.

"I'll try to understand. I really will, but I'm never going to like it. You are my only friend. I will always wish for you to be near me..." Gemma pulled away from Lilliana and clasped their hands together. "Tell me what I can do to help."

Lilliana knew she could count on Gemma. Elation filled her as she could envision how it would all work out. Now all she needed to do was give her all the details so she could do her part in the plan.

"I overheard my parents talking. I had no intention of listening until I heard my name spoken. I found out some interesting things that I never knew. Not the least being that Mama never intended to get married and Father had blackmailed her into agreeing to be his wife."

Gemma gasped. "What?"

"Makes you stop and question the validity of their love and all that doesn't it?"

Gemma's mouth hung open with shock radiating from her eyes. After a small pause while the information sank in she asked, "Why would he do such a thing?"

"Once upon a time Papa sailed his ship, the *Sea Rover*, as its pirate captain. Apparently he had a little feud with Mama's grandpere and she became the leverage he needed to enact his revenge. They came out of it okay, clearly as they are still together." Lilliana flipped her hand dismissively as she spoke. "The point is that Mama said that by the time I'm twenty if I still don't wish to wed, she planned on giving me the deed to the plantation in South Carolina."

Lilliana tried over and over to explain to her parents how much marriage was distasteful to her, without going into too much detail. If her father knew exactly how her heart had been bruised, he would have murderous intentions. The real issue was she didn't want anyone to know how naïve she had been. Now, she knew she could get what she wanted and nothing made her happier. Anxiety filled with equal swirls of excitement tumbled through her belly.

"That's still too long for me to wait. I won't be twenty until December and that is nine months away. What I want to do is sail there now and use my family position to gain control. My plans are not going to change just because nine months pass by."

"What good will that do? Without the deed securely in your control will they allow you to oversee the plantation? Isn't someone already there taking care of the property?" Gemma asked.

"There is an overseer yes. I'm hoping to convince him that the letter giving him orders to give me control got lost on the mail packet before my arrival. Come let's sit down in comfort as we work out the details." Lilliana grabbed Gemma's hand and led her to the settee. After they were seated she poured them both tea and handed a cup to her friend. Lilliana took a sip of tea before continuing their conversation. "I've thought a lot about what needs to be done. Even if the overseer doesn't believe I have control of the plantation no one has the authority to throw me off the property because it is owned by my family. If I have to wait, I'd rather do it in South Carolina."

Gemma nodded. "Okay, I suppose that makes sense. What do you need me to do?"

"Well the tricky part is leaving without letting my parents know. First, I need to find a ship sailing to America. Once I book passage I'm going to need a way to get my trunks on board without raising suspicion. I'm not worried about funds. I've been saving all my pin money for months now." Lilliana gave Gemma a smile. Surely she would see how she thought of every possible issue in her plan.

"So how do you plan on getting your trunks on board the ship?"

"That is where you come in. Once I know what ship I'm on, I'd like you to invite me to come stay with you in the country for a week." Lilliana set her teacup down and gave Gemma her full attention. She really needed Gemma to help her. If she didn't, her whole plan would fall apart. Her eyes pleaded with Gemma as she spoke, "My family won't question it because they know that our schedule is relaxed at the moment. It will give me a reason to pack a trunk or two and have them loaded onto a carriage. The carriage with your family crest on it that is."

"Oh, I understand. You will have the carriage drop you off at the docks and our servants will unload your trunks to be delivered to the ship. They won't have a reason to let your family know that you're boarding the ship. The servants will assume they already know." Gemma nodded her head in understanding.

"I knew you'd get it." Excitement filled Lilliana's voice. "It's all coming together now. I only have one little facet to figure out before I can iron out the rest of the details. The first item I need to cross off my list is to figure out what ships are heading to America and if they are accepting passengers."

"However are you going to figure that out?"

"Oh, that's the easy part. I will just ask Liam," Lilliana proclaimed.

Gemma blinked several times before she asked, "Won't he find that suspicious?"

"Not at all," Lilliana said waving her hand. "He's constantly talking about the Marsden shipping line and its competitors. He just started to take over the business. Our father believes it's time for him to learn about his future inheritance."

"I see. When do you plan on getting the information out of him?"

"Tonight at the Silverton's ball. Father is making him escort me. I will make sure to have a friendly conversation with him in the carriage on our way."

"You have thought of everything. I'm sure it will work just the way you want it." A small smile grew on Gemma's face as she looked at Lilliana. "I just wish your plans didn't have to take you so far away from England. Why couldn't you have fallen in love with a nice earl or baron...or even a mere mister? Anything that might inspire you to stay where I have an actual possibility to visit you, chances are I'll never be able to travel to America to visit. Promise me you'll come back to see me."

"I promise to come back to see you. In the meantime, we'll keep in touch with lots and lots of letters. I want to know everything about your life and when you find the man of your dreams."

"Good. I suppose I should go. I'll see you tonight at the ball."

Gemma stood up and grabbed her pelisse. After she donned it, she walked over and gave Lilliana a quick hug. She watched as Gemma left the room and got up to walk back to the window to look at the rose garden. All she could do at this point was hope all of her plans went off without a hitch. Doubts clouded her mind as she knew from experience nothing ever went exactly as planned, and naught could be done to alleviate her anxiety. Lilliana decided to try and let it go. She turned and left the sitting room to find some kind of diversion. Perhaps a book would work to distract her thoughts away from any possible problems—thinking, or over thinking in her case, had always been her worst enemy. With a smile on her lips Lilliana strolled to the library. Dark feelings would not sink through and ruin her good mood. Preparation was the key to success. No one planned and schemed better than Lilliana Marsden.

*R*andall Collins stepped out of a black open carriage and followed the Earl of Devon into his gentleman's club, Whites. Devon wanted to discuss business in a more dignified setting, hence the journey to his favorite club. Rand didn't much like overly pompous aristocrats, but Devon had an interest in a possible investment with his shipping company. If the meeting went as planned Rand would have a new investor and could expand his business.

"Ah, here we are, have a seat Collins and we'll discuss what is next for RandCo Shipping," The Earl said as he sat down in the nearest seat at the table. "And whether or not I want to give you some of my money to invest."

It grated on his nerves he had to seek investors to expand his business. Rand had a lot of big ideas and hoped the earl liked them enough to continue to invest in shipping company. He took the seat across from the earl and settled into discussing the future of his shipping company. With a small fleet of clippers at his disposal he did well enough for himself, but wanted to branch out into steamships for larger cargos and more reliable speeds.

"Did you have a chance to look over the papers with my proposal?" Rand asked.

"I did, and I admit my knowledge of shipping is rather limited. I hope you don't mind I invited someone that knows a bit more than I do to help me decipher some of the details. Viscount Torrington and his son should arrive soon." The Earl of Devon raised his head and scanned the room. He appeared to be scanning the room, as if looking for someone he invited to join them.

Irritation filled Rand's gut as he let the earl's words absorb deep into his mind. He clenched his fists tightly under the table, not wanting the man to see how much his words bothered him. Hell yes he minded, Devon could consult anyone he chose, it was his right after all to make sure he was doing the right thing for himself. However, he could have at least let Rand know they'd be meeting with someone else prior to arriving at the club. It was hard to be prepared for a meeting when all of the details hadn't been presented in advance. Before he could voice objection, two men walked in and took a seat at the table. One was as dark as the other was light. They bore a striking resemblance, in spite of the opposite coloring, that made Rand believe them to be closely related.

"Ah Torrington glad you and Liam could make it," Devon said. "This here is Randall Collins. He has grand ideas for steamships. What are your thoughts on the matter?"

As they had not been introduced, Rand gathered the older gentleman Devon spoke to was Torrington, the man he previously mentioned would be joining them. The upper class tended to refer to each other by their titles or last names. Rand couldn't wait until he could sail back to America. The higher born in English society had a snobbish attitude that he had trouble stomaching. Torrington nodded his head at both Rand and Devon before he started to speak, "Liam knows a bit more about steamships than I do. He has been looking into them for a while now to determine if they are worth investing in. I'm a clipper man, but I realize their days are numbered."

"I like the idea of steamships, but even they have their pitfalls. The coal needed to keep them running can be expensive. The cargo needs to bring in a more than fair price if a profit is to be made. They have their advantages, faster and more reliable travel. I think it's more economical for most cargo to continue to be brought over by clipper. Steamships are great for passengers and mail." The light haired man nodded at them as he sat up straight and looked Rand directly in the eye as he delivered his viewpoint.

It was obvious that Liam's beliefs were in direct opposition to his own. Rand clenched his hands into tight fists underneath the table as anger and frustration permeated his whole body. The boy probably had a point, although minute, Rand however did not want to deal in passenger ships. People made things messy. They could be demanding and irritating on a good day and damn abusive any other time. The chances of him being willing to start a passenger line bordered on slim to none.

"Is that the only good thing you can think of for steamships? What about cargo that requires a faster delivery? I know you English favor your tea. Steamships travel at faster speeds and allows for a swifter arrival. This means what you deem to be important cargo will arrive to its destination much sooner." He had to gain control of the conversation before these idiots talked Devon out of investing in his shipping line.

Steamships did make great passenger ships. The mail packets arrived much faster when they were placed on a ship powered by steam, but Rand had grander ideas. There were plenty of reasons to start investing in steamships. Those that began to do it sooner would have profits much sooner than those waiting to see if it worked. Sometimes it was worth it to take on a risky venture; although Rand didn't think it was as chancy as they were making it sound.

A bit of color formed on Liam's face. He clearly didn't like pointing out flaws in his estimation of the value of steamships. "You make a valid point, sir. Some cargo could benefit from the faster steamship. There is a clipper design that has been noted to bypass even a faster steamship. The record for the ship surpassed the fourteen knots of the steamship. That clipper managed to snatch up some of the tea trade. We had a few ships built around that design and they have worked wonderfully with any cargo that requires a more speedy arrival." Liam continued to glare at him as he spoke. His eyes crunched up in disapproval and his lips pursed into a thin line.

"Okay, I admit I'm just getting more confused the more these two gentlemen talk. Tell me straight Torrington, are steamships a good investment?" Devon asked.

"The short answer is yes, and no." Torrington grinned.

Torrington had an amused smile on his face as he watched his son sit back in displeasure. Apparently Liam's attitude entertained him or it could be the volley of their conversation back and forth, Rand didn't care to know what that something was though. He just wanted to derail them before they ruined his investment possibility. Damn them and their advice. If they kept talking about the negativities surrounding steamships they were going to talk the earl out of investing, and Rand would be right back where he started.

"That doesn't bloody help me." Devon threw his hands up in frustration.

"That's because there isn't an easy answer to your question. Any new venture is risky. All signs point to steamships eventually taking over. There are a few ships that are built to be powered by both steam and wind. We are having a few of those built to try out in our shipping line." Liam rested his hand on the table and tapped his forefinger on the polished wood as he explained, "The idea is that if coal runs out or becomes too expensive the option to use wind is still available and not all will be lost in the voyage. It will probably be a few years before we branch into a ship completely powered by steam."

"So you both do not believe steamships are the sound investment right now?" Heat began to dissipate through Rand as his anger reached a boiling point.

"In the future yes, but now it is still risky," Torrington said. "They are making a lot of progress in their designs, but they all have flaws. I'd go with what is a known quantity."

Rand unclenched his fists and wiped his sweaty palms over his thighs. His lips pursed in displeasure as he considered how to proceed. He couldn't erase the irritation from his voice as he spoke. "And yet you are still willing to try out a glorified clipper ship that could also be powered by steam?"

"Yes." Torrington continued with a bit of mockery in his voice, "I did say I leaned towards clippers at the beginning of the conversation."

Damned Englishman, and their perverse ways.

The conversation was spiraling out of control. Rand tried to steer the conversation in the direction he wanted, but they were relentless in their opinions. He curled his fingers into fists underneath the table and refrained from smashing them against the polished wood.

"I'll admit there is a certain beauty about clippers, but let's be realistic. The popularity of the ship has faded a lot over the past twenty years. The ship isn't seen in quite the same light as it used to be."

"So do you recommend investing or not?" Devon asked as he turned his attention once more on Torrington. "I need to give the man an answer."

Torrington looked at Devon and shrugged his shoulders. He looked him directly in the eyes as he spoke. "Honestly, it's up to you and how much of a risk you are willing to take with your money. It isn't a bad investment. No matter what, eventually you will make money." Torrington picked up his drink and took a quick swig. He set his glass back on the table and scanned the table before his eyes landed on the Earl. "To put it simply, Devon, it depends on the market and how well the cargo is managed. I did look over his plan and RandCo has been steadily gaining in capital. It just hasn't been at a rapid pace. Expanding at this juncture requires more money and it's not gaining enough on its own."

The more they opened their mouths the more irritated Rand became. He couldn't believe the gall of these men. They were talking around him instead of including him in the conversation. He had to force his way into it in order to be heard. He built RandCo all on his own. Yes, the progress had crawled at the pace of a snail, but the growth remained true. It might take him longer than he wanted it to, but he could continue to do it on his own. He'd be damned if he remained sitting here taking their distain and disapproval.

Rand forced his way into the conversation. "Good of you to give the stamp of approval on my business, Ol' Chap. Why don't I save you all the time and just say that the offer is off the table. I don't especially like being discussed like I'm not here."

Liam began, "We didn't mean to imply—"

Rand interrupted, "Save it. You act like I don't know a lick about business. I built this company all on my own without your expert advice. I can continue to assemble it without your money too, Devon. I admit the boost probably would have made expanding easier. I just don't like the strings that extra help apparently comes with."

He looked over and found Torrington studying him as if trying to ascertain his origin. He must not have a lot of experience dealing with Americans. He knew he could be a bit brash and defensive at times, but he had no desire to change.

"A bit hot-headed, aren't you." Torrington raised his eyebrows at him and a quirky smile lifted at the corners of his mouth.

"A product of where I happened to be raised, I suppose." Rand shrugged.

Torrington laughed before saying, "In America? Yeah, I suppose that could be the explanation. From my experience most of you could take a bit of lessons on diplomacy."

"And you all could learn to be more accepting of the differences in all men," Rand retorted.

"Down puppy. I meant no offense. My wife happens to be American. She can be a bit...stubborn at times. Don't do anything rash," Torrington reasoned.

Rand had to admit that little tidbit amused him some. Torrington's wife must be an exceptional woman to put up with his arrogance on a daily basis. It would be interesting to meet her and get a more in depth look at her character. "Your wife's American?

What state did she hail from? Maybe I know her family."

"Doubtful as they all died a number of years ago. Her plantation is being run by an overseer at present. It's located in Charleston, South Carolina."

"I never knew that," Devon stated.

"Yes, we're lucky it survived the War Between the States. She left shortly before the war broke out and sailed to France to live with her grandpere," Torrington explained.

"How ever did your plantation manage to survive the war?" Rand had to admit that he found it interesting that they had a plantation in Charleston that survived the war. A lot of the plantations had been burned to the ground by the Union army.

"Luck mostly." Torrington leaned back in his chair. "The union army decided to use it as a hospital. My wife, Pia, told her overseer to remain as neutral as possible and that allowed for a certain amount of leniency from both sides of the conflict."

"Well if we're done discussing business how about a bit of pleasure?" Devon asked.

"What do you have in mind?" Torrington questioned as he leaned forward and rested his hands on the table. "I have plans with my wife this evening and can't be drawn into anything too extensive."

"How about a game of whist?" Devon asked.

"I have to be back in a couple hours to take Lily to that ball." Liam looked at his father as he spoke.

Torrington nodded. "Good point. Lily has a temper and she isn't afraid to use it. Best if you're not late. Why don't you take the carriage home and send it back for me."

"I can always give you a lift back, Torrington," Devon offered. "Although I'm supposed to go to that blasted ball tonight too. Gemma is expecting me to escort her."

"As much as I hate to admit it, I think we'll have to attempt more amusing pursuits at a later date. Maybe tomorrow night?" Torrington looked to Devon for confirmation.

"Splendid idea." Devon nodded his affirmation. He turned towards Rand and asked, "Collins, you want to go to the ball?"

"Can't say I've ever been to a ball before. Sounds fun. I have a few days before I sail back home. It could be a nice diversion." Rand had been watching them discuss their options for entertainment. It resembled a pugilist in the ring; they volleyed shots back and forth at each other and danced around any real issues. If he hadn't been so irritated, he'd be a bit more fascinated by their way of speaking to each other. He never had any desire to go to a ball before, but he could add it to his once in a lifetime experiences.

"Good, good. Then just come with me to my townhouse. My valet can help you get ready and you can help me escort my daughter, Gemma."

Rand got up to follow the earl out of his club. He nodded at Torrington and Liam. "Nice meeting you gentlemen. Perhaps we'll see more of each other before I depart."

Pompous jerks. His real wishes didn't even come close to wanting to see them ever again. He knew he'd see them at the ball later that evening, but hoped it would be the last time he ever laid eyes on them. They single-handedly made him restructure his whole plan for expanding his business. He didn't hold them in any high esteem. The meeting did not go as he intended it to. These men and their grand ideas, or lack thereof, had made sure of that. No, what he felt for them bordered on hate. He had to deal with uppity men who believed they were better than him his whole life. A person didn't grow up in an orphanage without having some lasting internal scars. The emotional distress the high class brought out was deep rooted and he couldn't let go of it easily. In his experience they didn't give a damn for anyone, but themselves. These individuals were not different. If he never saw them again he might be able to forget their existence.

Thank you so much for taking the time to read
my book.

Your opinion matters!

Please take a moment to review this book on your
favorite review site and share your opinion with
fellow readers.

www.authordawnbrower.com

ABOUT THE AUTHOR

USA TODAY Bestselling author, DAWN BROWER writes both historical and contemporary romance. There are always stories inside her head; she just never thought she could make them come to life. That creativity has finally found an outlet.

Growing up she was the only girl out of six children. She is a single mother of two teenage boys; there is never a dull moment in her life. Reading books is her favorite hobby and she loves all genres.

BB bookbub.com/authors/dawn-brower

f facebook.com/1DawnBrower

twitter.com/1DawnBrower

instagram.com/1DawnBrower

Odds of Love (Dawn Brower)

Coming Soon

Believe In Love (Amanda Mariel)

Chance of Love (Dawn Brower)

Christmas at Fortuna's Parlor (Amanda Mariel and Dawn Brower)

Bluestockings Defying Rogues

When An Earl Turns Wicked

A Lady Hoyden's Secret

One Wicked Kiss

Earl In Trouble

All the Ladies Love Coventry

Coming Soon

One Less Scandalous Earl

Confessions of a Hellion

Marsden Descendants

Rebellious Angel

Tempting An American Princess

Coming Soon

How to Kiss a Debutante

Loving an America Spy

Marsden Romances

A Flawed Jewel

A Crystal Angel

A Treasured Lily

A Sanguine Gem

A Hidden Ruby

A Discarded Pearl

Novak Springs

Cowgirl Fever

Dirty Proof

Unbridled Pursuit

Sensual Games

Christmas Temptation

Linked Across Time

Saved by My Blackguard

Searching for My Rogue

Seduction of My Rake

Surrendering to My Spy

Spellbound by My Charmer

Stolen by My Knave

Separated from My Love

Scheming with My Duke

Secluded with My Hellion

Heart's Intent

One Heart to Give

Unveiled Hearts

Heart of the Moment

Kiss My Heart Goodbye

Heart in Waiting

Broken Curses

The Enchanted Princess

The Bespelled Knight

The Magical Hunt

Ever Beloved

Forever My Earl

Always My Viscount

Infinitely My Marquess

EternallyMyDuke

Kismet Bay

Once Upon a Christmas

New Year Revelation

All Things Valentine

Luck At First Sight

Endless Summer Days

Coming Soon

A Witch's Charm

All Out of Gratitude

Christmas Ever After